A CORNISH EVIL

THE LOVEDAY MYSTERIES

RENA GEORGE

ROSMORNA

INTRODUCTION

Loveday's boss, magazine publisher Merrick Tremayne, has married his housekeeper, Connie Bishop, in Truro Cathedral. But celebrations in an exclusive country house hotel come to an abrupt end when a woman is found murdered in one of the upstairs bedrooms.

Loveday's partner, Detective Inspector Sam Kitto, takes charge of the investigation. No one is allowed to leave the hotel. The situation is sensitive, but until his officers must interview everyone…even his friends are suspects.

As the hunt to find a killer spreads across Cornwall more distress is in store for the Tremayne family. Marietta Olsen, girlfriend of Merrick's half-bother, Cadan, has disappeared. Has she really taken herself off to a retreat as her parents maintain…or is something more sinister going on?

COPYRIGHT

Copyright © 2018 Rena George

The moral right of Rena George to be identified as the author of this work has been asserted in accordance with the Copyright, Designs and Patents Act 1988.

All rights reserved. No part of this publication may be reproduced, stored in a retrieval system, or transmitted in any other form or by any other means without
the prior permission of the copyright owner.

All characters and events in this book, other than those clearly in the public domain, are entirely the work of the author's imagination. Any resemblance to actual persons living or dead is completely coincidental.
***
Cover design by Craig Duncan
www.craigduncan.com/creative

CHAPTER 1

They had chosen Bach's inspiring *'Jesu, Joy of Man's Desiring'*, to accompany the bride's entrance into the cathedral. The soaring chords of the organ resonated all around as they moved past the rows of smiling wedding guests. Loveday stared at her bouquet and wished it would stop shaking. She was trying to focus on moving elegantly down the aisle to where Sam stood. She saw him turn and smile as she approached the altar and her heart did the little flip it always did when he looked at her like that.

She swallowed, wondering how this would feel if it was *her* wedding day. But it wasn't. Her friend Connie was the one getting married and right now she was gliding towards her man without a single trace of nerves.

Connie and Merrick were two of Loveday and Sam's dearest friends. They had been proud when they were invited to play the important roles of bridesmaid and best man at the couple's wedding in Truro Cathedral. Merrick Tremayne was the proprietor of *Cornish Folk* magazine. He was also Loveday's boss. Connie Bishop had been housekeeper at Morvah, the Tremayne family's converted farmhouse in Truro, for as long as Loveday could remember. She had long ago noticed the couple's easy way with each other and didn't miss the special looks that passed between them when they thought no one was looking. And now here they were – about to become man and wife. She stifled a sigh. Her friend looked amazing in the cream linen dress and matching coat she had helped her shop for. The gorgeous pale pink hat, encrusted with silk petals, had been the perfect complement.

The couple couldn't have chosen a more appropriate date to be married – February 14, St Valentine's Day. The cancellation of an event in the cathedral's busy diary made everyone feel it was meant to be. Loveday smiled back at the sea of familiar faces as she and Connie walked through the vaulted splendour of the cathedral. There were more guests than she had expected, particularly as she knew Connie had wanted a quiet affair, but judging by the blissful expression on the bride's face it wasn't a problem.

For a brief second, Loveday again found herself wondering how this would feel if it was her and Sam going through the wedding ritual, but it was a fanciful thought and she instantly dismissed it. They were happy as they were. Fixing her eyes on Sam's broad shoulders she moved with Connie to where the two men stood at the altar.

An hour earlier Loveday had been gasping with admiration as her friend floated down Morvah's impressive staircase and did a twirl at the bottom. 'Will I do?' Connie had asked in a small, nervous voice.

Loveday had handed her the bouquet of tiny pink and cream roses and smiled. 'You'll definitely do,' she'd said, ushering her out to the sleek black limousine waiting outside.

The same approval was now mirrored in Merrick's eyes as he turned to watch his bride's approach. Sam gave Loveday a wink, stepping aside to leave the bridal couple touching hands at the altar.

'I always cry at weddings,' her friend Cassie whispered, taking a tissue from her bag as Loveday slipped into the pew beside her and Cassie's husband Adam rolled his eyes. The organ fell silent and the great cathedral waited as the marriage service began. Loveday gulped back a lump in her throat. Cassie wasn't the only one dabbing her eyes as the couple repeated their vows.

Loveday glanced across the aisle to where Sam was keeping Merrick's elderly father Edward Tremayne company in the pew. She was surprised to see Sam's handsome profile looking so serious and wondered if he was remembering his own previous two marriages. The first one to Victoria, the mother of his two children, had ended in divorce. But Sam and his ex-wife had managed to retain a friendly relationship and he visited them often in their home in Plymouth. His second marriage had ended in tragedy when his beautiful young wife Tessa was killed in a road accident.

Loveday knew Sam still thought about her, perhaps he even still loved her. It was something she had no control over. She had learned to live with Sam's revered memory of his dead wife.

The cleric's voice, announcing Merrick and Connie were now husband and wife, brought her back into the vast space of the cathedral.

Cassie gave her a nudge. 'I think you're on again,' she whispered, nodding towards where the couple were being shown the way to the vestry to sign the marriage register.

Loveday blinked and took a breath, regaining her composure as she stood up and moved to Sam's side. Arm in arm they processed behind the bridal couple as a lone soprano began to sing *'Love Changes Everything'*, a romantic song Loveday recognized from a West End musical she and Sam had seen on a rare weekend in London. She couldn't suppress her smile. Knowing Merrick's fondness for musicals she had no doubt whose choice this had been.

CHAPTER 2

Merrick hadn't stinted on the reception. He'd booked the Trevere Manor Hotel, on the outskirts of Truro. It was one of the most luxurious and expensive hotels in Cornwall. Not that Loveday was complaining, and judging by the delighted look on Connie's face, she wouldn't be raising any objection to the sumptuous venue either.

The special entrance for the bride and groom had been festooned with cream and pink roses. These had been entwined with green and silvered foliage. Loveday and Sam looked at each other and smiled when they saw Connie's gasp of delight and watched her reach up to kiss Merrick, her eyes shining.

'Merrick's pushed the boat out with this place,' Sam said, lowering his voice to a whisper as his arm encircled Loveday's waist. 'Look at the room through there.' Opulent was the word that came to mind as Loveday peeked into the beautiful dining room. Chandeliers glittered above tables draped in white linen and beautifully set for the wedding breakfast. Each table had a centrepiece of cream roses and an array of long-stemmed wine and water glasses sparkled at each place setting.

Connie saw their admiring glances as she and Merrick came

forward to join them. 'Isn't this perfect?' She beamed, leaning in to kiss Loveday's cheek.

Loveday sighed. 'It's spectacularly beautiful. How clever of you Merrick, to plan all this by yourself.'

'Exactly what I was thinking,' Connie said. She had a twinkle in her eye.

Merrick's hands came up in a gesture of defence. 'OK…OK, I can tell you two have seen right through me.' He hesitated. 'I hired a wedding planner.'

'A wedding planner?' Connie's eyebrow arched. 'You hired a wedding planner after we agreed to keep the wedding low key?'

Merrick gave an uncertain frown. 'I wanted it all to be perfect.'

Loveday and Sam held their breath, hoping they weren't about to witness the happy couple's first row. But a slow grin was spreading across Connie's face as she held out her arms to embrace Merrick. 'That's the most endearing thing I've ever heard,' she said.

'So, I'm forgiven for doing all this despite what we agreed?'

'You're forgiven.' Connie laughed.

'I think your guests are arriving,' Sam said.

Within minutes the room had filled with buzz and chatter as the wedding guests mingled and waitresses bearing trays of drinks moved amongst them.

The hotel manager had guided Connie and Merrick to a little table bearing the two-tier wedding cake on a silver tray. There was a burst of applause as the couple made the ceremonial first cut with a silver knife and everyone looked on as they posed for the photographer.

'They look so happy Sam, don't they?' Loveday said, tilting her head to the side as she watched them. He didn't reply and when she glanced up at him she saw the faraway look was back in his dark eyes. Did this mean he still resented his first wife Victoria was planning to marry again? Or was the wistful gaze for his beloved Tessa? Loveday guessed the second, and a shiver ran through her.

The arrival of a waitress with a tray of champagne forced her mind back to the present. The next time she looked at him, Sam was smiling. He seemed happy for now and that was good enough for her. 'This is the kind of marriage that's for keeps,' he said as she sipped her champagne and nodded agreement. 'Connie and Merrick are perfect for each other.'

'They do look good together,' a voice over her shoulder said. When Loveday swung round it was Edward Tremayne's craggy face she saw smiling back at her. 'It's good to know Merrick has found someone lovely. I've been reminiscing about the first time Connie came to us at Morvah.' He sighed. 'We couldn't have found a better housekeeper. And she cooks like an angel.'

'And now she's one of the family.' Loveday laughed.

But Edward's eyes had strayed across the room to where his younger son, Cadan, stood with a beautiful young woman. 'That's his latest girlfriend, Marietta Olsen,' he said. 'She's a student at Falmouth Art School.' His old face creased into a grimace. 'They're sleeping together, you know,' he muttered, his body language registering his disapproval.

Loveday saw Sam give the couple an appraising look and knew the same thought she'd had was crossing his mind. The girl looked to be still in her teens, while Cadan was in his thirties. She was far too young for him. She also looked a lot less sophisticated than his usual choice of lady friend. Cadan must have been aware they were discussing him for he swung round and flashed them a dismissive smile. Marietta too, had noticed them and leaned her head in towards Cadan, no doubt enquiring who they were. Loveday smiled at the girl, but she could well understand Edward's disapproval. She hoped the young woman knew what she was doing getting mixed up with Cadan Tremayne.

She was remembering her first encounter with Merrick's half-brother on the stairs at the magazine office in Truro some years ago. She had been going up to the editorial floor to be interviewed for the editor's job on *Cornish Folk*. Cadan had barred her way, teasing her about being in a hurry. She hadn't appreciated being accosted by a complete stranger who'd been arrogant enough to try flirting with her. Learning later he was a member of the Tremayne family had done nothing more to impress her. She was still annoyed his behaviour had almost spoiled her delight at having been offered the job as Merrick's right-hand woman at the magazine.

She saw Cassie waving to her from the other side of the room and nodded back, returning the wave. She would have preferred to have been seated at a table with Cassie and Adam, but as best man and bridesmaid she knew she and Sam would be placed at the top table with the bridal party. Out of the corner of her eye she noticed Cadan move across the room. She watched as he tapped one of the waiters on the shoulder. The man wheeled round, a look of dismay on his face when he recognized Cadan. Loveday frowned, it looked like they were having words. She wondered what was going on there. She knew Merrick's half-brother wasn't popular, but this was something else. They were definitely arguing. These two had history. She glanced away, deciding it was none of her business what Cadan got up to.

She hadn't noticed Priddy Rodda come up beside them and spun round at the sound of her voice. 'Has Sam got his speech ready? I'm expecting a few laughs,' her friend joked. Loveday had no idea what was in the speech. Sam had been very secretive about it. She pulled a face. 'I did offer to help but he insisted on writing it on his own. I don't know what's in it, but judging by the tiny scrap of paper he composed it on, it won't be long.'

'Suits me.' Priddy's ample chest rose in a satisfied sigh as she raised a glass of sherry to her lips. Judging by her rosy glow Loveday guessed it perhaps wasn't her first glass. She smiled. Priddy wasn't used to alcohol, but she seemed to be enjoying it.

'Look.' Priddy nodded to the hotel manager, who had made

his way to Connie and Merrick and was having a discreet word with them. 'I think this chap is going to tell us to go through and take our seats at the tables.' Loveday thought so too. She put her glass on a nearby table and gestured to Sam that she was disappearing to the ladies' room for a few minutes. 'I'll come with you,' Priddy said, keeping her glass with her as she followed Loveday through the room and out across the hotel foyer. As they passed the stairs to the upper bedrooms a man came running down, casting anxious glances about him as he went. His jeans, tee shirt and scruffy looking black leather jacket appeared so out of place there that Loveday hesitated, turning back to watch him as he took long hurried strides across the plushly carpeted foyer and went out through the revolving glass doors.

Under different circumstances she might have followed him out to the car park to see which way he went, but this was Connie and Merrick's wedding reception and the running man was none of her business. A movement from behind made her glance round. Another guest had emerged from the wedding room and appeared to edge back round the corner as the man passed her. There was no mistaking the filmy peach dress. It was Cadan's friend, Marietta and it very much looked like she hadn't wanted to be spotted. But who exactly had she been hiding from?

Loveday was still puzzling over the girl's odd behaviour when she and Priddy got back to the others. 'Oh look. There's Cassie and Adam,' Priddy said. 'I think I'm at their table. I should go and join them.' She gave a departing wave as she hurried off across the room, leaving Loveday looking around her. The top table people were still on their feet and Sam and Merrick were chatting. Connie appeared at her side. 'I know it's ridiculous but I'm as excited as a schoolgirl today,' she said. 'I'm feeling guilty now I ever suggested our wedding should be a quiet affair. Merrick was right. This is wonderful.'

'It is,' Loveday agreed, catching Connie's gaze to her impeccably dressed wedding guests, who were now filing through and organizing themselves at the cluster of large round tables. She could see a group of waitresses gathered by the door with bottles of champagne ready to come in and fill everyone's glass. 'I think we should take our seats,' she said.

The Trevere Manor Hotel had excelled itself with the wedding breakfast menu. Loveday ran her eye down the list of enticing choices.

Trevere Poached Salmon with Cucumber and Dill
Cornish Oyster
Artichoke Royale with Truffle and Pear

* * *

Rosemary and Cornish Sea Salt Roasted Belly of Pork
Roast Rib of Cornish Beef and Mustard
Grilled Looe Bay Mackerel
Cornish Goat's Cheese Tart
Roast butternut squash, asparagus, tender stem broccoli, Chantenay carrots

* * *

Bread and Butter Pudding with Rodda's Clotted Cream
Cornish Trifle
White Chocolate Mousse with Raspberries and Lime
A selection of Cornish biscuits and cheeses

'WHAT! NO CORNISH PASTY?' Sam said, picking up his menu card. Loveday gave him a nudge.

The food was as delicious as it promised. Loveday saw Connie glancing over the tables and knew she was assessing how much their friends were appreciating the banquet. There was no doubt they were. It was excellent, even if it did lack Connie's special touch.

Sam's speech got an enthusiastic reception and she noticed a few hankies coming out when he threw in a few off the cuff remarks about the couple. Sam clearly knew things about their friends that even she hadn't. Loveday led the applause when he'd finished and Merrick and Connie beamed across the table at him as he sat down.

'Where did that come from?' Loveday said in a conspiratorial whisper over the rim of her glass. 'It was brilliant.'

Sam gave her a smug smile. 'I can rise to the occasion when it's called for, besides, I'm quite fond of these two.'

Loveday stretched across to squeeze his hand. 'I know you are,' she said. 'We both are.'

The band struck up a rendering of *'You're My World'* as Merrick led Connie onto the dance floor and a ripple of applause went around the room.

Loveday glanced to Sam. 'You know of course we are expected to join them now?'

'I didn't,' Sam said as he got to his feet and held his hand out to her. 'But I'll give it a go. I'll try not to step on your toes.'

It was another hour before Merrick and Connie slipped away to prepare for their departure.

'I think they were hoping to get off without any fuss,' Loveday said to Sam, keeping her eye on the stairs as everyone waited for the couple to emerge.

'There's no way that was going to happen,' Sam said. He and Adam had returned to the reception after loitering suspiciously around the back of the couple's going away car.

'Please tell me you two didn't tie strings of cans and a *"Just Married"* notice to the back bumper of Merrick's car,' Cassie said, giving her husband a suspicious look.

'I think it's exactly what they've been doing.' Loveday grinned.

A cheer went up as Merrick and Connie reappeared and made

their way to their car. Everyone followed. A tear sprang into Loveday's eyes as she and Sam hugged them both.

Edward was also looking emotional as Merrick threw his arms around him. There was even a hug for Cadan and Marietta. A roar of laughter went up as the car moved off trailing a clatter of cans and red L sign.

Cassie shook her head. 'Classy,' she said.

Sam and Adam shared an amused look as they all headed back to the room and the band began to play a slow waltz.

CHAPTER 3

'There's always an anti-climax after the happy couple leave,' Priddy said, looking wistful as she followed the others back to their table.

The band had started up again and Adam gave Priddy a funny little bow and indicated the dance floor. 'What do you say, Priddy? Shall we put this lot to shame?' He had a twinkle in his eye.

Priddy's cheeks pinked up as she laughed. 'But nobody else is dancing.'

'They will once we get out there,' he said, holding out his hand to her.

Loveday flashed a smile to Cassie. 'I'd say that was doctor's orders, Priddy.' The old lady flushed with pleasure and put her hand into Adam's. He led her onto the dance floor as the music changed to a more upbeat number.

'She's right though, isn't she?' Cassie said, watching her husband and her old friend glide across the floor. 'Things do go a bit flat after the bridal couple leave.'

Sam put down his glass and grinned at her. 'Is that your coy way of begging me for a dance?' Cassie got to her feet. 'I thought you'd never ask.' She smiled at Loveday. 'You don't mind if I pinch your man for a while?'

Loveday raised an amused eyebrow. 'Not if you return him in one piece.' More couples were taking to the floor and the atmosphere was picking up again. Loveday's eyes went around the room. Everyone seemed to be enjoying themselves. It had been a lovely wedding. Her gaze came to rest at the doorway and the figure there she recognized. She frowned. It was Detective Sergeant Will Tregellis! Now what was doing here – and looking so agitated as his eyes scanned the room? Loveday guessed he was looking for Sam, and a flash of annoyance shot through her. Even a detective inspector surely deserved a day off for his best friend's wedding?

She followed his gaze and saw it connect with Sam's. The men exchanged a coded nod. Loveday's brow creased into a deeper frown. Will had definitely come to take Sam away. He continued dancing with Cassie until the music stopped. Even she could tell something was going on as he escorted her back to their table and asked her and Loveday to excuse him.

Cassie threw a quizzical look to her friend and Loveday nodded to the door where Will was still standing. He was looking increasingly concerned. The two men had their heads bent together in serious conversation as they moved out of sight into the hotel's reception area.

Cassie leaned across the table and lowered her voice. 'What's going on?'

Loveday's eyes were still on the open door. 'I'm guessing it's something serious. Will Tregellis wouldn't turn up here to report a burglary. Looks like Sam might be called away.'

Adam and Priddy had got back to the table as Sam came striding across the floor.

'I'm sorry everyone. There's been a…' He hesitated. 'There's been an incident. I'm afraid I have go.' He threw Loveday an apologetic look. 'I really don't have any choice. I need to check this out.'

Loveday nodded. 'Don't worry about me. I'm sure I can cadge a lift home.'

'Of course. Come back with us,' Adam cut in, but he was looking serious. 'Is there anything I can do, Sam?'

'No, it's fine, thanks. The police surgeon is on the way.'

Loveday's head snapped up. 'You mean it's here? Whatever this incident is has happened right here in the hotel?'

Sam's mouth compressed into the familiar hard line she knew so well. 'Please don't ask me anymore, Loveday. I don't know any details yet.' He glanced to Adam. 'Actually, there is something you could maybe do. The rest of my team is on the way and we'll be asking everyone to remain here. If you could assist them by making sure no one leaves the room.'

'Of course.' Adam's expression was grim.

'What about us, Sam?' Loveday asked. 'What can we do?'

'Keep everyone calm until we know what we're dealing with. For now it's better if things carry on as normal down here.'

Loveday didn't miss the confused look passing between Cassie and Priddy.

'Do you think somebody has been murdered?' Priddy whispered, as they all watched Sam stride away.

'I'M SO sorry calling you away from your friends like this,' Will said as he and Sam hurried up the hotel stairs. 'But I knew you would want to know.'

'Where's the body?' Sam asked as they reached the first landing.

'She's along here. Room 125.'

A uniformed officer was outside the door, a man Sam recognized as the hotel manager by his side. He looked like he was trying to contain rising panic as he stepped forward. 'I'm Frederick Manning. I'm the hotel manager.'

Sam nodded, indicating he should stand back as Will opened the bedroom door. The forensic team was already inside taking pictures and sweeping the room for fingerprints and any other clues they could find. Sam wasn't hopeful. Hotel bedrooms would be full of fingerprints.

One of the forensic officers looked up. 'If you could give us a few minutes more, Inspector. There's not much room in here.'

Sam could see the victim's slippered feet protruding from the far side of the bed. 'We'll need this whole corridor sealed off, and all these rooms checked,' he said.

The manager's worried frown deepened, but he nodded his consent.

'Are any guests currently in their rooms on this floor?'

'No, the rooms have all been checked,' Will said. 'These rooms all appear to have been allocated to wedding guests who are staying overnight, and they're all downstairs at the do.'

'Was our victim a guest?' Sam asked, hoping she wasn't one of Merrick and Connie's friends.

The manager came forward. 'As far as we know she had nothing to do with the wedding. This is the only single room on this floor, and the lady only checked in today.'

'Do we have a name?'

Will took out his notebook. 'Rebecca Monteith, at least that's the name she gave when she checked in.'

'Exactly what time was this?'

Will checked his notebook again. 'According to the receptionist, it was shortly after ten, although they were rather busy with preparations for the wedding reception.'

'I presume she had a case with her?'

'There is a leather overnight bag in the room.'

Sam swung round to face the manager. 'Do you know how many nights she booked?'

Frederick Manning dragged his eyes from the door of the room. 'Only the one night as far as I know.'

It was another ten minutes before Doctor Robert Bartholomew, the Home Office pathologist, arrived with his usual bluster. 'Why can't you organize these things with a bit more consideration, DI Kitto?' He threw an exasperated frown at Sam as he swept past him. 'And why are these places always so claustrophobic?'

'Sorry, Robert.' Sam couldn't hide his grin. He knew the man's bark was worse than his bite. 'We'll try to do better next time. Did we interrupt your lunch?'

Robert Bartholomew scowled and turned his attention to the forensic officer as he moved away from the body.

'Is it all right for me to examine it now?'

'Yes, it's fine, doctor. We've done as much as we can here.'

'What about putting my bag on the bed?'

The forensic officer nodded.

'Right,' he puffed, getting down on his knees with some difficulty. 'What do we have here?'

Sam held back, giving the pathologist as much space as the small crowded room afforded. He hoped they might at least get some clues from this initial medical analysis of the body. Having waited ten minutes as Bartholomew went through the basic procedures, Sam cleared his throat and enquired, 'Any first impressions?'

The pathologist looked up from the body, a thermometer in his latex gloved hand, and sighed. 'I'm not a clairvoyant.'

Sam gave him a pleading look. 'Anything would help, Robert.'

'OK, what about this? Our lady here is standing by the window and her killer comes in.'

'Why would they have a key?' Will asked.

'I don't know.' The pathologist shrugged. 'Perhaps the door wasn't locked.'

'You mean the meeting could have been arranged?'

'You're the detective, Sergeant Tregellis. I'm just a lowly pathologist.'

Sam ignored the remark. They were used to the man's scathing quips. He knew his job and that was what was important. He glanced to the door. It clearly hadn't been forced. 'OK,' Sam said. 'Either the door wasn't locked, or the victim opened it and invited her killer in.' His eyes went around the room. 'There's no sign of a struggle, so the victim probably didn't feel threatened. It could have been a pre-arranged meeting.' He paused, the possible options running through his mind.

'Let's say the victim was comfortable about meeting whoever killed her. Well, she must have been. It's hardly normal to invite people you don't know to your hotel room.'

Will nodded. 'Doesn't really get us any further though, does it?'

It didn't and at this stage of an investigation Sam knew it wasn't helpful to be making assumptions. He looked over the pathologist's shoulder, trying not to retch at the sight he saw. There was blood everywhere. The victim was on her back, in the cramped space between the bed and the window, her dead eyes staring at the ceiling.

'So much blood,' Sam said. 'Does this mean she didn't die instantly?'

'Not necessarily,' the pathologist said. 'Depends what the knife went through on the way in. We'll know more later.'

'What about the murder weapon?' Sam asked.

'Too early to say. Some kind of survival, bush craft type knife perhaps. Like I said, I'll know more when I get her on the table, but the wound doesn't look ragged, so I would be surprised if a serrated edged knife was used.'

The officer leading the forensics team was packing his case. 'Whatever kind of knife they used, they didn't leave it behind,' he said, glancing about him. 'We've been over every inch of this room.'

Will was trying to avert his eyes from the horror in the room. 'They'll have got rid of it by now anyway,' he said.

Sam grimaced. 'Probably,' he agreed, as Robert Bartholomew got awkwardly to his feet, complaining about his stiffness.

'We'll take her away now,' Bartholomew said, motioning to the undertakers at the door to move in.

Sam stepped out into the corridor and beckoned the hotel manager over.

'We'll be removing the body now. Perhaps you could make sure no wedding guests or members of staff are in the reception area. My officers are already down there.'

All colour drained from the man's face. 'Will you be taking the elevator? There is a way through the kitchen allowing you to avoid the public areas.'

'OK, we'll do it that way.' Sam had no wish to alarm Merrick and Connie's friends and family any more than they must already be.

LOVEDAY RECOGNIZED the two detectives on Sam's team as they set about taking statements and collecting names and addresses from the wedding guests. Adam had positioned himself at the door, advising anyone who wanted to leave the room to first check with the police officers. Some people had already left, but Loveday knew Sam would want a list of everyone who had been present in the hotel that morning.

'It's definitely a murder,' Priddy said, folding her arms and giving a knowing look to the approaching figure of Detective Constable Amanda Fox. Loveday knew the woman who was striding towards them. She had an abrasive attitude that didn't make her one of Loveday's favourite people. But then she knew there was no love lost from Amanda's direction either. She made no secret of her displeasure at Loveday's relationship with her boss.

'Well now, ladies,' DC Fox said, putting her clipboard on the table and sitting down as her eyes travelled to Cassie, Priddy and Loveday in turn. 'I'll need everyone's address.' She clicked her pen on and made notes as each of them spoke. 'I need to interview each of you separately,' she said, lifting her head and looking directly at Loveday.

'Is it a murder?' Priddy persisted, not able to disguise the excitement in her voice. 'Is it one of the guests? Do you think we might know them?'

'I'm afraid I can't discuss it with you,' Amanda said, pushing a handful of ginger curls from her face.

'Well there's no point interviewing me,' Priddy said. 'I don't know anything. I haven't seen anything suspicious here.'

'Did you leave the room at any point?'

Priddy was about to say no, and then remembered she and Loveday had slipped out to the ladies before taking their seats for the meal. She told Amanda this, adding, 'But I didn't see anything unusual.'

'What about you, Mrs Trevillick?'

Cassie shook her head. 'Same as Priddy. What exactly do you want to know?'

Amanda shrugged. 'Anything you want to tell me.'

'There's nothing. We'd all been having a lovely time until you people turned up.'

Loveday saw a flicker of annoyance cross the detective's face as she switched her attention to her.

'And you, Miss Ross? What can you tell me?'

Loveday was remembering the man she'd seen dashing from the hotel when she'd followed Priddy to the ladies' room.

'It's probably nothing,' she began. 'But I do remember seeing a scruffily dressed man coming down the stairs into the reception area.' She raised her eyes to the ceiling, trying to recall the incident. 'It would have been about two hours ago, before the staff began to serve the meal.'

'Can you describe this person?'

'About five foot eleven, forty-something, short white crew cut hairstyle, jeans, grubby white tee shirt, old black leather jacket.'

'Not one of the wedding guests then?'

Loveday shook her head. 'I've never seen him before.'

Her attention was drawn to the nearby table where a worried looking Edward sat with Cadan and Marietta. She was remembering how the young woman had stepped out of sight when the scruffy man hurried past and out of the hotel. Should she tell Amanda or think more about this first? It could have been her imagination that Marietta hadn't wanted to be recognized by the man.

'Let me get this straight.' Amanda's interest seemed more focused now. 'You're saying you saw a man hurrying down from the upstairs bedrooms and leave the hotel?'

'I don't know what he was doing upstairs, and I didn't say he was hurrying.' Loveday knew she was being awkward, but the woman irritated her.

Amanda's shoulders stiffened. She didn't like being corrected. 'So, he wasn't hurrying?'

Loveday pursed her lips. 'I suppose he was. He wasn't running or anything like that, but he was moving smartly.'

'Could you describe him to a trained officer? It would be helpful to have an e-fit.'

'Of course,' Loveday said. 'I'll do everything I can to help.' She wished she knew what it was she was being asked to help with.

CHAPTER 4

'How much longer do you think they'll keep us here?' Priddy said with a sigh.

Loveday and Cassie exchanged an amused look.

'I thought you were enjoying this,' Cassie said.

'Not enjoying…no.' Priddy sounded indignant. Then she smiled. 'But it was kind of exciting when all these police people moved in and started questioning us.'

'And what if it really does turn out to be a murder they're investigating?' Loveday said.

'D'you think that's what it is?' Priddy asked, leaning forward, her normally cheerful blue eyes now concerned.

'I think so,' Loveday said.

Priddy clapped her hands to her hot, plump cheeks. 'I never thought it through. You mean some poor soul could be lying dead in one of those bedrooms upstairs? But that's awful.'

'It's beginning to freak me out too,' Cassie said. Adam was still keeping guard by the door and he smiled across at her.

Edward Tremayne's weary expression caught Loveday's attention again. He was still sitting with Cadan and Marietta at a nearby table.

Priddy had followed her gaze. 'Poor old gentleman,' she said. 'He looks all in. This isn't the way his son's wedding day should have ended. Can't you speak to Sam, Loveday, and persuade him he should be sent home?'

'I expect we'll all be allowed to leave once the detectives have taken a statement from everyone.' She nodded across the room to where the officers had gathered in a corner and appeared to be comparing notes. 'It looks like that might not be too far off,' she said. A side door into the function room opened and Sam came in. He looked across to Loveday and her friends and gave them a brief nod as he made his way to check on his team, and beckoned Adam to join them.

She watched as they stood in a huddle, heads nodding. And then Sam turned to address the room. He put up a hand to silence the expectant murmur from the wedding guests.

'I apologize for having to keep you all here,' he said. 'But I hope you understand my officers had to take statements from everyone. Your assistance and patience has been much appreciated.'

'Does that mean we can go?' Edward Tremayne's expression was hopeful.

'It does, sir. And thank you again for your understanding.'

Cadan jumped to his feet. 'Is that it?' he demanded. 'Are you offering no explanation for keeping us all penned up like animals for more than an hour?'

Marietta tugged at his sleeve, clearly urging him to sit back down, but Cadan was in his stride now.

'Well, Inspector Kitto?' he persisted. 'What do you say?'

'We are investigating a serious crime…sir.' Loveday could see Sam was struggling to contain his temper. 'We understand how inconvenient detaining you here might have been but like I said, your co-operation has been appreciated.'

'For heaven's sake, man.' Cadan sighed. 'Has there been a murder or not?'

Loveday saw the colour drain from Marietta's face. She looked as though she wanted to flee from the room. Edward was also looking distressed. He clearly didn't like his son's confrontational behaviour. Loveday strode across to their table, aware every pair of eyes in the room was on them and touched the elderly man's arm.

'I'll ask the staff to bring your car to the door, Edward,' she said, firing a scowl in Cadan's direction. 'I think you should take your father home now.'

'Yes, let's go home,' Marietta said. 'Your poor father looks exhausted.'

They were all on their feet. Loveday leaned in to Edward and whispered in his ear, 'Forget about all this police stuff. It was a gorgeous wedding. Merrick and Connie did us all proud.'

The old man nodded and Loveday was heartened when she saw his face stretch into a craggy smile. 'It was a lovely wedding, wasn't it?'

'It certainly was, Edward,' she said, linking arms with him as she walked with the group to the door.

ADAM, Cassie and Loveday dropped Priddy off at Storm Cottage before continuing along Marazion seafront to where they lived. They parked in the wide drive between the large house and Loveday and Sam's cottage.

'Come in and have a drink,' Cassie said. 'Sam probably won't be home for hours yet.'

All Loveday wanted to do was to kick off her heels and put the kettle on, but she relented and followed them into their large, warm kitchen where the table was set for tea. A young woman Loveday recognized as the daughter of a friendly couple who lived in the village, appeared at the door and smiled at Cassie. 'I was just going to put a pizza in the oven for the children. There's plenty if you want to join us.'

'No, it's fine, Ginny,' Cassie said. She turned to Loveday. 'You know Ginny? She's Colin and Sal Macey's daughter from up in the village.'

Ginny and Loveday smiled at each other.

'It's all very quiet around here,' Cassie said. 'Where are the children?'

Ginny nodded through the house. 'In the playroom watching Harry Potter.'

Cassie smiled. 'I'll check on them.'

Excited squeals came from the playroom as Sophie and Leo greeted their mother.

Loveday grinned. 'What a welcome. They'll come racing through here any second to find you too, Adam.'

He gave a happy nod. 'Homecomings are always special. I think we should go and grab a drink before all hell lets loose in here.' But Adam didn't have a chance to pour their drinks before the children bounded in. He threw his arms wide to them. Loveday was also given an excited hug as Cassie got out her phone to replay the video she'd taken of the wedding.

'Aw…' Sophie gave a disappointed scowl. 'The bride isn't wearing a wedding dress.' She looked up at her mother. 'Why is she not wearing a wedding dress?'

'Brides can wear whatever they like,' Cassie explained gently.

The little girl didn't look impressed. 'When I get married I'm wearing a wedding dress,' she said firmly.

Ginny came into the room and hovered uncertainly by the door. Judging by the appetizing aroma drifting through from the kitchen the pizzas were ready.

'I think Ginny has your tea on the table.'

'Is it pizza?' Leo asked. 'I only eat pizza.'

'Would you believe it's pizza?' Ginny said, ruffling the children's hair as they trooped past her on their way to the kitchen.

'I'll pour those drinks now,' Adam said, smiling after the children. 'What would you like, Loveday?'

'Anything, so long as it isn't fizzy. There's only so much champagne a person can down in one day.'

Adam poured three small glasses of brandy and handed them round before taking a seat beside his wife on the large leather sofa.

Cassie dropped her head back onto it. 'At least Merrick and Connie were spared knowing their wedding was hijacked by…' She frowned. 'Well, we don't even know by what. All Sam said was it was a serious incident.'

Adam stared into the toffee-coloured contents of his glass and frowned. 'It's a suspicious death. I'm sure Sam won't mind my telling you. It will be public knowledge soon enough.'

'You mean murder?' Cassie said.

'That will depend on what the post mortem reveals, but on the face of it I would say so, yes.'

'Has Sam said any more to you, Loveday?' Cassie asked.

'No, nothing, but then I've hardly spoken to him. He's had his hands full with everything that's been going on.'

Cassie took another sip of her brandy. 'What was that you were telling the female detective about seeing a man on the stairs?'

Loveday shrugged. 'I only mentioned it because he looked so out of place in such a swanky hotel. We were all in our finery and he was in jeans, tee shirt and a rather grubby leather jacket.'

'You mean he was coming down from the bedrooms?' Adam said.

'I don't know. It's what Amanda Fox assumed.'

'She's probably right,' Cassie said. 'I've stayed in the hotel. It was years ago admittedly, but there are no public rooms upstairs, only bedrooms.'

The door, which had been left ajar, was pushed open as Sophie and Leo came in, a little less boisterously than before.

'Good pizza?' Cassie enquired, smiling from one child to the other.

'Yummy,' Sophie said, rubbing her tummy.

Ginny had followed them through. 'I can stay a bit longer and get these two off to bed if it helps,' she offered.

'Can she, Mummy?' Sophie was clearly excited about the idea. But Leo, at seven years old, was more hesitant.

'We can get ourselves off to bed,' he said, huffily.

'Of course, you can, but it was kind of Ginny to offer. Say thank you to her,' Cassie said.

'No need for thanks. We enjoyed ourselves,' Ginny said, beaming around the room.

'Well, thanks anyway. We're very grateful to you.' Cassie got up and walked with Ginny to the door.

Loveday could hear Ginny protesting in the hall and smiled. No doubt Cassie was pressing some notes into the young woman's hand for the child minding.

When she came back into the room Loveday was on her feet. 'I'll be off too. Thanks for the drink,' she said, gathering up her things. 'I need to be at home when Sam gets back.'

'And here was me thinking you wanted to stay and bath these two before getting them off to bed,' Cassie teased.

Loveday saw Leo's look of horror and she held up a hand. 'Don't worry, Leo, it's not going to happen. You two are far too energetic for me to cope with.'

His relieved smile was so obvious that everyone laughed.

'Keep us in the loop about Sam's body, won't you,' Cassie said, walking with Loveday to the door.

'I'm not sure he would describe this as *his body*.' Loveday laughed. 'But I know what you mean. Sam's not in the habit of sharing the gory details of his case, but if there's any fresh news then you and Adam will be the first to know.'

Loveday went out and crossed the yard to her own cottage, running her hand over the bonnet of her beloved white Clio, which was parked in the drive. She let herself into the kitchen and looked around her. The colourful mugs were still there on their hooks, the dishes from their hurried breakfast that morning still on the drainer by the sink. It all looked so comfortingly normal. She sighed, depositing her bag on the table. Her life was continuing as normal when the body of some poor unidentified soul lay in the city mortuary. She was trying to shake off a feeling of sadness as she went through to run a bath.

It had been Loveday's intention to sit up in bed with her treasured copy of Daphne du Maurier's *Rebecca* and wait for Sam to come home. She knew he wouldn't share the details of the investigation but sometimes he mentioned things to get her slant on events and she was curious to hear more about it. He'd rung earlier, warning he could be late, so despite her best intentions she was fast asleep by the time Sam got home and crept quietly into the cottage.

It was dark when Loveday woke next morning and squinted at the luminous face of the clock. It was just six. She turned and wrapped herself around Sam's warm body and wondered if he'd been glad she hadn't been awake when he'd got in last night. Had he been relieved he'd been spared having to answer her questions? She hoped not. They were a team after all, but she knew he didn't like her getting too involved in his cases. He told her it was to keep her out of the firing line, but Loveday suspected the truth was he didn't appreciate what he sometimes called interference.

She slipped out of bed, wondering if she could chance taking an early jog along the front. She didn't want to return and find Sam had already left for work. On the other hand, he looked so peaceful sleeping there. She smiled. Poor Sam. He had probably crashed out exhausted last night, or possibly in the early hours. She went to find her tracksuit.

The sharp, damp air hit her as she opened the kitchen door and stepped outside. She rubbed her hands over her arms and stamped her feet in the drive. Cassie and Adam's house was in darkness. Like all sensible people the family would still be curled up in bed on a Sunday morning. She questioned her sanity, jogging along a beach road while the rest of the world slept, but she had always found it an invigorating experience, especially when she had Marazion to herself. Loveday paused at the top of the drive, listening to the soft sounds of the morning. She could hear the slap of the waves against the sea wall and knew it must be high tide. She closed her eyes and tried to picture the cobbled causeway to St Michael's Mount under water. It made her shiver. The street lamps cast pools of yellow on the frosty footpath as she took off in the direction of the bird reserve, her breath coming out in cloudy bursts.

Loveday allowed her thoughts to drift back to the previous day and to the discovery of the body in an upstairs room of the hotel. Much as she had tried to put aside any suggestion it had marred the celebration of Merrick and Connie's big day, she knew it had put a damper on it.

Marietta's lovely face floated into her mind and she wondered if the girl had told Amanda Fox about seeing the running man. She would ask Sam about that. Suddenly she was anxious to be back at the cottage.

Sam was stirring when Loveday crept past the bedroom to have her post jog shower. It was her way of mentally cooling down after the efforts of running. She couldn't imagine starting a day any other way. By the time Sam was awake she was showered and dressed and had brewed a pot of strong coffee. She looked up as he wandered into the kitchen, tying his dressing gown.

'Good sleep?' she asked.

He rubbed his eyes and made a lazy stretch. 'Mmm...I did. I was flat out.' He wrinkled his nose. 'That coffee smells good.'

Loveday filled a mug and handed it to him. 'We could all have done without yesterday's horrible events. Have you made any progress?'

He sat down and sipped the strong, black coffee. 'To be honest, I'm not sure. We don't even know if we have the right name for the victim.'

'I didn't realize you had an identity.'

'Only the name she registered with at the hotel.'

'So, are you going to tell me?' Loveday said, refilling her coffee mug.

'Rebecca Monteith.'

She screwed up her face. 'Monteith? It sounds familiar.'

Sam was suddenly alert. 'You know her?'

'Maybe. I'm not sure.' Loveday held up a hand. 'Let me think.' The name was running through her mind…someone from the past…someone she had interviewed perhaps? She slapped her hand on the table. 'Now I remember. It was a Rebecca Monteith who verified the sketches Priddy donated to the Penzance Museum.' She looked at Sam. 'The ones Priddy's neighbour, old Jago Tilley hid in his shed and bequeathed to Priddy in his will before he was murdered. Don't you remember?'

Sam nodded. She could see his mind working. 'They were sketches of Jago's mother as a girl by one of the famous Newlyn artists, Walter Langley.'

Loveday gave him a surprised look. 'Well remembered,' she said. 'Apparently Jago's mother lived next door to Langley and she used to pose for him.' She frowned. 'I hope your victim is not Rebecca. She was a nice woman.'

'Do you know anything more about her?'

'I can find the feature I wrote about her, but in a nutshell I remember she had an upper-class Edinburgh accent, was an elegant forty-something at the time I interviewed her, which was a few years ago. She was also a volunteer at the cathedral. She worked in the gift shop.'

Loveday was staring across the kitchen. 'You know, it's funny,' she said. 'You imagine an art historian would be all dour and serious, but this woman couldn't have been more different. She was working at the gallery in Penzance Museum cataloguing the exhibits.'

She blinked. 'I've just thought of something. There's a connection between her and Cadan's girlfriend.'

'What connection?'

'Art of course. Rebecca is an art historian. Marietta is an art student at Falmouth College.'

Sam's brow creased into a frown. 'You've lost me,' he said. 'What does Marietta have to do with any of this?'

Loveday glanced away. It was only now she realized she should have told Amanda Fox about Marietta's suspicious behaviour when the scruffy man passed her in the hotel reception. She thought she'd been protecting the girl. Now she would have to explain herself.

She took a breath. 'I'm assuming you've read all the witness statements your team took yesterday from the wedding guests?'

Sam nodded. 'I was coming to that. You saw some scruffy individual in the hotel reception.'

'It was a bit more than that, Sam. He was coming down the stairs and seemed to be in a hurry. I mentioned him to Amanda because I thought he looked so out of place.' She hesitated, biting her bottom lip. 'The thing I didn't mention was that Marietta saw him too. I could be wrong, but I got the impression she didn't want him to see her.'

Sam's face darkened. 'And you didn't mention this to Amanda? Why on earth not, Loveday?'

Loveday shrugged. 'I don't know. Sorry. But I'm mentioning it now. Anyway, I'm sure Marietta would have put this in her own witness statement.'

Sam stood up and put his empty mug on the table. 'There is no mention of this man in the girl's statement. We need to speak to her again.' He turned to Loveday. 'I believe you're going in to help with an e-fit?'

She nodded.

'Good,' Sam said. 'If you can get down to the station early then we can take the finished image with us when we call on Marietta Olsen.'

CHAPTER 5

The Sunday traffic on the chilly February morning was light as Loveday drove behind Sam's grey Lexus into Truro. She had never before been asked to provide police with an e-fit of a suspect. It felt strangely important. She spent the journey trying to focus her mind on the man she'd seen in the hotel the previous day. He was quite distinctive, but would her recollection transfer into a useable image?

Loveday was feeling unusually nervous as she accompanied Sam into the police station and was directed to a small room. She didn't recognize the female officer who sat by a computer and gave her a welcoming smile, indicating she should take the seat beside her. She watched fascinated as an image of the man she'd seen began to take shape on the screen.

'The nose was a bit bigger and thinner…more chiselled,' Loveday said. 'And the eyes were closer together and smaller. They could have been grey, certainly light coloured.'

She watched the image change as the officer included each new bit of information.

'His hair was bleached white, very short…like in a crew cut,'

Loveday said, tilting her head to examine the emerging face. 'Can you make the cheekbones a touch higher and more pronounced?'

'Like this?' the officer asked, making another adjustment to the image.

Loveday's eyes lit up as the image changed again. 'That's him,' she said, pointing. 'He's the man I saw.'

The officer smiled. 'Well done. We'll get this circulated.' She stood up. 'If you could wait here for a moment, I think DI Kitto would like a word.'

She was either unaware of Loveday and Sam's relationship, or she was being discreet. It didn't matter. She gave her a nod as she went out of the room.

By the time Sam showed up a few minutes later Loveday's positive mood had grown.

'I'd like to come with you to see Marietta,' she said.

She had been expecting an immediate refusal, but Sam had pressed his lips together in the way he did when he was considering something.

'We won't be going to Falmouth to see Marietta until later today because Will is currently checking out another line of enquiry. It wouldn't be appropriate for you to be present when we interview a witness.'

Loveday suppressed a frown. She doubted very much if Marietta had gone back to Falmouth. She would more likely be at the Tremayne house with Cadan and Edward.

She got to her feet. 'I was planning to drop by Morvah to see how Edward is today. He looked pretty exhausted at the reception. I want to make sure he's all right.' She slid him a look. 'We could go together.' It wasn't a lie. She had planned to check up on Merrick's father. If Marietta and Cadan also happened to be there, then how could Loveday have known?

Sam was giving her a curious stare and she knew he was aware of her line of thought even though he made no mention of it. 'We'll take my car,' he said.

Morvah was a beautiful old farmhouse on the edge of Truro that Merrick and his father had restored and extended as their family home. The fields surrounding it also belonged to the Tremaynes, although Loveday knew these were leased off to a neighbouring farmer. Neither she nor Sam knew what kind of car Cadan was currently driving, but she thought the low slung green sports number parked by the side of the house looked like his style. She didn't miss Sam glance at it as they pulled up by the steps to the front door.

The woman who admitted them to the house was a stranger to them. It felt odd not being greeted by Connie, but Merrick mentioned he had engaged a temporary housekeeper to look after Edward while he and his new wife were on their honeymoon. 'We've come to see Mr Tremayne,' Loveday said as the woman stood back allowing them to step into the vast hall.

'We have two Mr Tremaynes. Which one would you like?' the woman said pleasantly.

'Both of them are home?' Sam asked.

The woman nodded.

'It's Mr Edward we've come to see,' Loveday said quickly.

'Who is it, woman?' a voice from across the hall called out.

The woman gave an irritated cluck. 'He knows my name is Molly. Molly Murphy,' she said in her engaging Irish lilt. 'He's being awkward.'

'It's Sam and Loveday,' Sam called out. 'Can we come through, Edward?'

'What a lovely surprise,' Edward said, appearing from the big sitting room and coming forward, his arms outstretched to greet them. He gave Molly an exaggerated scowl as he passed. 'What are you doing, woman, keeping my friends out here in the cold?'

Molly gave a hopeless shrug. 'See what I mean?' She turned to Loveday with a wink. 'The man's impossible.'

Loveday held back to have another word with the housekeeper as Sam followed Edward into the big comfortable front room. She suspected Molly and Edward were closer than either of them was letting on. 'Am I right in thinking you and Edward are friends?' she asked.

'Acquaintances,' Molly said. 'The banter between us is all in fun. I've known Connie for years and when she asked me to look after Edward while she and Merrick were away I was more than happy to step in.'

Loveday laughed. 'I can see Edward is in good hands.' She turned, still smiling, as Molly headed for the kitchen, and she went off to join the men. 'Well,' she said, sinking into the chair on the other side of the blazing log fire from the old man. 'Have you heard from the happy couple yet?'

EDWARD NODDED. 'Merrick rang me this morning. He and Connie are having a wonderful time on Corfu. Of course, they don't yet know about the terrible business after they left the reception yesterday. They don't need to have their precious holiday spoiled.'

Loveday gave a wistful smile. 'I'm glad you didn't tell them, Edward. Well, not yet anyway.'

'I wish that young hothead, Cadan, shared your opinion,' Edward said. 'He's been pestering me for Merrick's contact number. Why the young whippersnapper wants to spoil his brother's honeymoon is anyone's guess.'

Loveday saw Sam's brow descend into frown. She wondered if he was agreeing with the old man, or could his expression mean something else? She stared at him. Did Sam think the dead woman was somehow linked to Merrick, or even Connie? She hoped he wasn't planning to suggest they should cut their honeymoon short and return home.

The door opened and they all looked up as Molly came briskly into the room carrying a tray of tea things. 'I know you didn't ask for it, but these poor people looked like they needed some sustenance,' she said.

Sam leapt to his feet to relieve her of her heavy burden and placed the tray on a coffee table.

To Loveday's amusement she saw Edward's eyes twinkle. 'Thank you, Molly,' he said.

The woman flushed and bustled off, muttering she was only doing her job. But before she reached the door Cadan burst into the room, with a timid looking Marietta trailing behind him.

'Bring two more cups, Molly.' The instruction was fired at the woman's back as she passed him and went out the door. Edward glowered at his son's rudeness, but Cadan ignored the look.

'Well now,' the new arrival said, giving Sam an insolent stare. 'What have we done to deserve a visit from the constabulary?' He flicked his attention to Loveday and then back to Sam.

'That's none of your business, Cadan,' Edward snapped. 'Our friends need no excuse to drop in.'

Cadan had flung himself into a chair, but Marietta was still on her feet, apparently unsure what to do.

Loveday smiled at her. 'Come and join us, Marietta.'

Sam got to his feet, offering his chair to the girl. She sat down.

'Have you come to tell us who got themselves murdered yesterday?' Cadan asked.

Edward rolled his eyes and his head shook in a gesture of exasperation at his son's brash behaviour.

'It's all still under investigation,' Sam said stiffly.

'But someone was murdered?' The question came from Marietta and they all turned to her.

'Nothing has been confirmed yet. We're still waiting for reports,' Sam said.

Edward sighed as Loveday moved forward to pour the teas. 'It's all very sad,' he said. 'We could have done without that upset at Merrick and Connie's wedding.'

Loveday put a cup and saucer on the table beside Edward. She glanced at Marietta. 'You looked quite distressed by it all yesterday,' she said. 'Are you feeling better now?'

'It's not pleasant being questioned by the police,' Marietta said.

'I hope my officers were sensitive in how they dealt with things,' Sam cut in.

'Oh, I didn't mean to suggest…' Her voice trailed off.

Loveday saw Cadan scowl at the girl from across the room and quickly interrupted. 'I know what you mean, but I guess any information the police can gather at the start of an investigation is valuable.' She was aware of Sam's eyes on her and knew he would be wondering where this was going.

'I suppose so,' Marietta conceded. 'It doesn't stop you feeling like a criminal.'

For a second no one spoke and then Sam said, 'Why would it make you feel like a criminal, Marietta?'

She shrugged. 'I don't know. I didn't mean that. It was a stupid thing to say.' But she was avoiding Cadan's eyes.

Loveday waited a beat and then said, 'I had to help the police this morning. They wanted me to make an e-fit of someone I saw.'

Marietta's eyes widened. 'What do you mean, someone you saw?'

'I was walking through the hotel foyer before we all sat down for the meal and I saw this man coming down the stairs. I noticed him because of his unkempt appearance. He looked out of place.' Loveday was aware Sam had fixed his gaze on Marietta.

'Being unkempt isn't a crime,' Marietta said.

'It is in my book,' Cadan interrupted, reaching for one of the tiny cakes Molly had brought in with the tray of tea things.

'Anyone who goes about like a tramp should be arrested on sight,' he said, grinning at Sam.

'Do we know who this person is?' Edward asked.

Sam's eyes were still on Marietta. 'Not yet,' he said, sipping his tea. 'But we should find out soon.' He fished the e-fit composite image from his pocket and offered it to Edward. 'This is him.'

Edward took the e-fit and studied it. He shook his head. 'It's not anyone I know.'

Sam retrieved the picture and handed it to Marietta. 'What about you? Did you see this man around the hotel yesterday?'

Loveday saw the colour drain from Marietta's face, but she shook her head. 'I don't know him.'

Cadan glanced at the picture and frowned. 'Looks like a nasty piece of work to me. What was he doing at Merrick's wedding?'

'We don't know he was at the wedding, only that he was in the hotel,' Sam said.

'Well, good luck with finding him, whoever he is,' he said, getting to his feet. 'Marietta and I have better things to do with our weekend and as she has to get back to Falmouth in the morning, we plan to make the most if it.'

'You're studying art, I believe?' Sam said.

Marietta nodded. 'That's right, at Falmouth School of Art.' She smiled and for the first time since she had entered the room her face came alive. 'I love it,' she said.

Loveday stood up with her and handed the girl her card. 'Next time you're in Truro and fancy a girly chat,' she said, watching the girl slip the card into the pocket of her long green skirt, 'give me a ring. We can have coffee.'

She was aware of the frown crossing Sam's face and avoided his eyes. She was only offering the girl a coffee.

As Cadan and Marietta crossed to the door, it opened and Molly appeared with two cups and saucers on another tray.

'You're leaving?' She looked from one to the other. 'I thought you wanted tea?'

'That was ten minutes ago.' Cadan gave her a frosty look. 'You'll have to do better than this if you want to go on working here.'

Molly shrugged. 'Please yourself,' she said. Loveday thought she'd caught the quiver of a smirk on the housekeeper's face as she turned to leave the room.

'Since when was it your decision who we hired and fired around here?' Edward's face was dark with anger.

Cadan wheeled round to confront him. 'You're too soft with people, Father. If you don't keep them in line they will walk all over you.'

'Like you try to do with Merrick and me?' Edward snapped. 'You're only here because Merrick stood up for you when you asked to move in, but don't think for a minute we can't see through you.'

Loveday could see Marietta's flush of embarrassment at the family spat and saw her place a delicate hand on Cadan's arm. 'We should go, Cadan,' she said softly.

Cadan sighed and shook his head as he and the girl left the room.

Edward turned to Sam and Loveday. 'I apologize for my son's behaviour. You shouldn't have had to witness that. Cadan can be impossible at times.'

'All families have their differences, Edward. I shouldn't worry about it,' Sam said. But Loveday could see he too was furious with Cadan.

'No, don't make excuses for him. I know my son all too well. He only comes back to Cornwall when things get difficult for him elsewhere. I know he's broke and people are pursuing him for money.' Edward sighed. 'Not that there's anything unusual about it. Cadan always has money problems. I only wish he could show a bit more respect for those trying to help him.'

Loveday moved to clear away the tea things, but Edward waved an arm to stop her. 'Leave it. Molly will come flying in here scolding me if you do her job for her.' He smiled. 'Now there's a lady who stands for no nonsense. She's the one who can keep Cadan in order, which is probably why he kicked off. I believe Molly takes pleasure in winding him up.'

'So long as she looks after you properly,' Loveday said.

Edward smiled and settled back in his chair again. 'She clucks like an old hen, but her heart's in the right place.'

'We'll leave you to Molly's tender mercy then.' Sam grinned as Loveday came forward to plant a kiss on Edward's cheek. She put another one of her cards on the low table beside him. 'I know you will have my number somewhere but keep this at hand in case you need me.' She stood back, smiling at him. 'If you have any problems at all, Edward, then please call me, either you or Molly. I can be here in minutes.'

The old man raised his eyes to meet hers. 'You know Merrick, Connie and I all regard you two as family.'

Loveday nodded fondly at him. 'That's exactly what we are, Edward,' she said, putting an arm around Sam's waist and drawing him close. 'We're family.'

Loveday was bracing herself for a ticking off from Sam as they left the house. Inviting Marietta to ring her had been a gesture of friendship. The girl didn't give the impression she had many friends. She knew Sam would argue that Marietta might be involved in his investigation but it was no reason not to befriend her.

They'd got as far as the car when Sam's mobile rang. He fished it out of his pocket and glanced at the name on the screen. 'Yes, Amanda?' he said.

Loveday watched his eyebrows shoot up as he listened to what the young detective was saying.

'I'm on my way back now,' he said briskly. He ended the call and turned to Loveday. 'We've identified your unkempt man,' he said.

'And?' Loveday waited expectantly.

'He's one of us. He's a cop.'

CHAPTER 6

*L*oveday had been thinking about her e-fit man as they drove back to the city centre to collect her car from the magazine office. She turned to Sam. 'Who was it that recognized your man?'

'It wasn't one of the team, if that's what you're thinking. Amanda circulated the e-fit on the police computer. Somebody from the Met recognized him and got in touch.'

'Do you know what he was doing in Cornwall?' Loveday was thoughtful.

'I'm not sure. We'll check it out when I get back to the station.'

'Does he have a name, this man?'

'Victor Paton. Detective Sergeant Vic Paton.'

Loveday's brow wrinkled. 'I wonder if he's here working undercover?'

'No, according to Amanda's informant our man is no longer on the Force. He left under a cloud apparently. I don't have any details yet.'

'What about Marietta?' Loveday asked. 'You didn't ask her if she knew the victim.'

'I haven't forgotten about Marietta. The reason I didn't ask her was because we have not definitely confirmed the victim's identity. When we do, and if there could be a connection with the college at Falmouth, then I will obviously be speaking to Marietta again.'

Loveday nodded. She didn't want to pursue the conversation about Marietta any further in case the girl did actually contact her. For the moment at least Sam didn't seem to be bothered about that.

When they reached Lemon Street, he pulled up outside glass doors of *Cornish Folk* magazine and Loveday leaned across to plant a kiss on his cheek before getting out of the car. For a while she stood on the deserted pavement watching the Lexus move slowly up the hill before she turned and let herself into the office.

The building was deserted. Even the cleaners who came in on Sunday morning had been and gone. Loveday ignored the lift and ran up the stairs to the editorial floor. She hadn't planned to be in the office today, but since she'd had to come to Truro anyway for the e-fit she decided to take the opportunity of calling in. Her time wouldn't be wasted, because there was always something to do here.

She'd thought to finish off an article she was part way through writing about a flower farmer down in West Cornwall. But she found herself typing the name Victor Paton into the computer instead. Her eyes widened as the information appeared on the screen. According to what she was reading, the man appeared to be a private detective who ran a business from an address in Falmouth. Loveday stared at the screen. There was no picture of him, so she couldn't definitely confirm that this was the same man she'd seen at the hotel, but it seemed more than likely. Loveday clicked on the magazine's archives and scrolled through the list of articles until she found the one she had written about Rebecca Monteith. She printed it off and made herself a cup of coffee in the editorial's tiny kitchen before going back to her desk to read through it again.

She remembered the day she'd gone to the Penzance Museum to interview Rebecca. She'd tracked her down to a small room off one of the upper galleries. She'd been behind a table covered in sketches and charts. Loveday remembered how the woman had looked up and smiled at her over huge black-rimmed spectacles as she came into the room.

'Ah, you found me,' she'd said. 'Not many people know about my little garret up here.' She'd got up and come round the table to shake Loveday's hand. 'Sorry about the other day. The cathedral gift shop can be a bit hectic, particularly at this time of year. I shouldn't have suggested it as a meeting place.'

Loveday hadn't minded. In fact she'd been rather pleased because since the meeting had been rearranged she could see Rebecca in her own environment. She remembered how much she had enjoyed trailing after the woman as she went around the gallery, logging each valuable painting in turn and making notes about it as she went.

One painting in particular had captured Loveday's interest. It was an enormous watercolour of distraught women weeping by the quayside of a Cornish fishing village and Rebecca had explained that the painting depicted the aftermath of a disaster at sea where the women were waiting for news of whose husbands had survived and whose had perished.

The painting by Walter Langley had been entitled *Among the missing – Scene in a Cornish fishing village, 1884.*

It had given Loveday the opportunity she'd been seeking to bring up something else she felt Rebecca Monteith could help her with.

There had been a murder in Marazion. An old fisherman by the name of Jago Tilly, who happened to live next door to Priddy Rodda, had bequeathed her a couple of sketches of his mother that Walter Langley had drawn many years before. Loveday had taken photographs of them intending to ask Rebecca if she thought they were genuine. The original sketches had been with the police. Rebecca had examined Loveday's photographs and believed the sketches really were works by Walter Langley.

And she'd been right. They had subsequently been valued at several thousand pounds. However Priddy had decided not to sell them and donated the sketches to the museum. As far as Loveday knew they were still on display there in Penzance.

She sighed, reading through the article again and allowed her mind to drift to the Falmouth Art School and Marietta. Could the two women have known each other? Could Rebecca have been connected to the art school? It was certainly possible.

Loveday finished off the dregs of her coffee and folded the pages of the article with the printed details of what she'd found online about the private eye in Falmouth. She washed her cup and went back to the computer to finish off the flower farm article.

It was an hour later before she locked up the office and went to find her car in the staff car park.

The roads were still quiet, but Loveday wasn't in any hurry to get back to the cottage, so a detour via Falmouth wouldn't be too much out of the way. She had typed the postcode of the private detective's office into her satnav and had set off from Truro feeling unexpectedly excited.

The Falmouth Detective Agency appeared to be in the front room of a run-down basement flat in a property behind the shops in the town's main street. Loveday left her white Clio in the waterfront car park. There were quite a few other vehicles there and she'd wondered if one of them belonged to Victor Paton. Strolling through Falmouth on a bleak Sunday afternoon was evidently more popular than she had imagined, for quite a few people were out and about. She decided it was a good thing because she wouldn't feel quite so conspicuous skulking around the Falmouth Detective Agency. It wasn't exactly an obvious business. In fact, unless you knew it was there you could very easily miss the place. Loveday walked past it several times, not wanting to appear to be loitering. She had no idea why she was taking pictures of the place on her mobile, but it seemed an opportunity not to be missed, even though the property looked deserted. Seeing the place had told her absolutely nothing.

She found a nearby cafe and sat at a window looking out across Carrick Roads as she sipped her hot drink wondering what connection Victor Paton could possibly have had with the posh country house hotel where Merrick and Connie had held their wedding reception. Her brow creased as she mentally re-lived the time when she'd seen him hurrying down the stairs. Had he been visiting someone in one of the bedrooms? She put down her cup. Had he had been visiting Rebecca? She bit her lip, frowning. Could Victor Paton be the person who murdered Rebecca? The thought made her heart skip a beat. And what about Marietta? She was sure the girl had recognized the e-fit of Victor Paton. Once again her mind returned to the incident in the hotel reception when she'd seen Marietta draw back around a corner for fear the man might see her. What did that mean? Should she discuss all this with Sam or would he accuse her of meddling in his business? She drained her cup and pushed it away. She was drinking far too much coffee.

THERE WAS no sign of Cassie's big green Land Rover in the drive when Loveday got back to Marazion. She guessed the family would be enjoying a day out together. Perhaps they had gone to another seaside resort for Sunday lunch? Loveday wasn't in the mood for her own company. She parked outside the kitchen door but didn't go into the cottage, instead turning back and strolling along the front to Priddy's home. The afternoon was getting darker and as Loveday got closer to her friend's cottage she was pleased to see lights on. Priddy answered her knock and gave her the welcome she knew to expect from her friend.

'Come away in, my lovely,' Priddy said, drawing Loveday into the cheery warmth of Storm Cottage. 'I've just put some scones in the oven, you couldn't have called at a better time.'

Loveday smiled. It seemed to her Priddy was always either putting something in the oven or taking something out. Either way she wasn't complaining. Apart from a slice of toast she had shared with Sam before they left for Truro that morning, Loveday realized she hadn't eaten all day. And it was now almost 4 o'clock.

Her friend's fat black cat gave Loveday an ominous look as she walked into the kitchen. She knew she was about to be shifted from her comfortable armchair by the fire.

'Sit down, my lovely,' Priddy said. 'I'm sure a cup of tea wouldn't be going wrong.'

'Sounds perfect.' Loveday smiled across at her friend as she warmed her hands by the crackling log fire.

Priddy put on the kettle and shushed the cat from its chair.

'So, tell me how your Sam is getting on with his investigation,' she said, setting out cups, saucers and tea things.

'I honestly wouldn't know. He doesn't confide in me.'

A look of disappointment crossed Priddy's face. 'What nothing? You must at least know if it's a murder.'

Loveday took a breath, wondering how much she should tell Priddy. It was probably public knowledge already. She looked up. 'Can you promise me to keep this strictly under your hat, well at least for the time being?'

Priddy nodded and Loveday could see the excitement creep into the old woman's cornflower blue eyes.

'It is murder then?' Priddy said.

Loveday nodded. 'It looks very much like it.' She paused. 'The woman who died had signed herself into the hotel as Rebecca Monteith.' She watched Priddy's face, waiting for the realization to dawn.

When it did, her friend stared at her open-mouthed.

'Rebecca? You mean the same Rebecca who verified old Jago's sketches of his mother?'

Loveday pulled a face. 'Possibly. Sam's not certain, but the victim signed herself in the hotel register as Rebecca Monteith.'

'But surely it wouldn't be difficult for Sam to confirm it? I mean Rebecca Monteith is very well known hereabouts. Anyone connected to the Penzance Museum for instance would be able to tell him who she was.'

Loveday had been thinking about this. Priddy was right. It would be very easy for Sam to confirm this, he probably had done by now. If he had checked out the feature she'd written for *Cornish Folk,* then Rebecca's picture was there. If this really was the Rebecca Monteith they knew then it would have been obvious to Sam and his team by now.

Priddy was staring at her. 'Why would anybody want to kill such a lovely woman?'

'I don't know, Priddy. I guess that's what the police have to find out.'

'What about this strange man you told the woman detective you saw in the hotel? What's Sam thinking about him?'

'I don't know.' What she had discovered about Victor Paton was definitely something she couldn't share with Priddy or anyone, not at the moment. 'I suppose Sam will have to do some digging to find out about him,' she said. 'I was asked to go to Truro Police Station this morning to help make up an e-fit.'

Priddy frowned. 'What's that?'

'You know what an e-fit is, Priddy. It's when a witness helps a trained officer to construct a likeness of a suspect. It's all done on a computer.'

'Oh,' Priddy puffed out her cheeks. 'In my day it was an artist's impression. Not that such sketches were ever accurate. How can anyone concoct a picture of someone a witness may have seen for only a few seconds?'

Loveday sipped her tea and said nothing. But somebody had

recognized the e-fit. Somebody had named him as Victor Paton, ex-Metropolitan police officer. It was her own assumption that he was the same person who ran the Falmouth Detective Agency.

Priddy got up to take a tray of scones from the oven and slid it onto the worktop before transferring them to a wire rack to cool. She popped two of them onto plates for herself and Loveday and brought them to the table. 'We'll probably get indigestion eating them when they are as new as this, but never mind. It's worth it.' She pushed the butter dish towards Loveday. 'You'll need lashings of this. Don't skimp on it now, your figure can stand it.'

Loveday laughed as she split the scone in two and spread the butter. She took a bite. 'Delicious, Priddy,' she said her mouth full of scone crumbs. 'You're always feeding me up. You must think this is the only reason I come to visit you.'

Priddy shook her head and her plump pink cheeks wobbled. 'I wouldn't mind if it was, but I know it's not. In fact if you're not expecting Sam back till late, I could cook properly for you.'

'I couldn't possibly impose on you,' Loveday said, but the idea appealed to her. Sam would undoubtedly not get back before midnight. That was the usual pattern in the early days of a case. 'Well only if you let me help,' Loveday said.

Priddy smiled. 'Don't worry, my love, you'll be doing most of the work. Now, how does a steak pie sound? I only made it this morning but there's far too much for only me. You'd be doing me a favour if truth be told.'

The mention of steak pie took Loveday back to the Scottish Highlands, and the Hogmanay meal she and Sam had shared with her family when they'd been on holiday there at Christmas. Had that been only two short months ago?

CHAPTER 7

The night was black and bitterly cold as Loveday walked home along the seafront feeling comfortably full after Priddy's homely steak pie supper. She hadn't expected Sam to be home until late, but he'd texted her saying to expect him around 9 o'clock. She just had time to light the fire before he was due to arrive. She had debated with herself whether or not to put a match to the kindling. There hadn't seemed much point for the two or three hours before they went to bed that night, but the little sitting room felt cold and unwelcoming without the cheeriness of a log fire sparking in the grate.

The room was warm and cosy by the time she heard him come in the back door. She got up and went to meet him, helping him off with his thick tweed coat. 'I had a meal at Priddy's earlier, but I can stick something in the oven if you haven't eaten.'

Sam shook his head and gathered her into his arms. 'We got a takeaway at the station.' He made a face. 'It was pretty horrible, but it filled a space.'

She led him through to the fire and sat him down on a chair. He sank gratefully into it. 'I'm bushed,' he said. 'It feels like we've been chasing our tails all day.'

'So you're no further forward with the case?'

Sam rubbed his eyes hard and blinked. Loveday could see how tired he was.

'We did get the victim's ID confirmed.' He looked at Loveday. 'I'm afraid it was Rebecca.'

Loveday sat down in the chair opposite. 'I'd more or less expected that.' Her gaze went to the fire and the flames licking over the logs she'd put on earlier.

'I was hoping we might be wrong about it being Rebecca,' he said. 'But there's no mistake. Sorry.'

They sat for a few moments without speaking, staring into the fire and then Loveday stood up. 'How about a mug of cocoa?'

'I'll settle for a large Glenmorangie if you'll join me.'

She was already on her way to the kitchen to find the whisky bottle. Moments later she was back with two glasses of their amber-coloured drinks.

Sam had moved to the sofa and held out an arm for Loveday to curl up beside him.

She snuggled up and watched him sip his whisky. 'Why would anyone want to kill a sweet woman like Rebecca?' she asked, shaking her head. 'She was just about the most harmless person anyone could imagine.'

Sam put down his glass and stretched. 'Who knows why anyone gets murdered. Someone had it in for her, that's for sure.'

'So you think it was premeditated?' Loveday asked.

'Probably. Our killer had brought a knife with them after all. Unless it was normal for them to carry a weapon around. Who knows?'

Loveday was thoughtful. 'Could it have anything to do with her work, do you think? Maybe it was someone who didn't agree with one of her valuations.'

'I doubt it,' Sam said. 'You don't kill somebody because your painting isn't as valuable as you thought.'

'No, that's not what I meant. What if she had told someone

their painting was not original, that it was worthless in fact? Now, if the owner of the painting had wanted to keep the fact a secret and Rebecca was the only one who knew the painting wasn't the real thing...' She paused. 'Well, wouldn't that be a motive for killing her?'

Sam blew out his cheeks. 'It's a theory, but hardly a very likely one.'

'Have you discovered any more about Victor Paton?'

'We know he's a private eye and has a place in Falmouth,' Sam said. 'We haven't tracked him down yet.'

'Private eye?' Loveday repeated. She had no intention of mentioning her own earlier visit to Falmouth. 'So what would a private eye have been doing at the hotel? Do you think he could have been visiting Rebecca?'

'We don't know. It's one line of enquiry. We have to find him first. We're still looking.'

'Does that mean you have somebody watching his place in Falmouth?'

'That is for me to know and for you not to,' Sam said.

She knew he was thinking he'd said enough for one night, but she had one more question. 'What about Marietta? Did you see her again today?'

Sam shook his head. 'We'll visit Marietta in Falmouth tomorrow, hopefully when she's out of Cadan's clutches.' He got to his feet, pulling her with him. 'And that, my darling, is my last word on the business.' He wrapped his arms around her and kissed the top of her head. 'Bed is calling,' he said.

IT WAS STILL dark next morning when Loveday jogged along the seafront, but there was a newness in the air, the start of a fresh day. It was the time she enjoyed most. She did all her best thinking on the morning jog. It was quite possible during these morning jogs for her to plan the day ahead, even work out the format for any interviews she had lined up. That morning, however, the only thing on her mind was Rebecca. She couldn't get the image of her in the Penzance Museum out of her head.

She could still see her lowering her huge black-rimmed spectacles and smiling up at her the day she had gone to interview her. There had been a picture of Rebecca in the article Loveday had produced for the magazine and she was confident this was how Sam and his team had identified her. Another image was coming into her mind. Once again she could see Marietta drawing back into a corner that day in the hotel as the man they now knew as Victor Paton came hurrying past her. She had clearly not wanted to be seen by him, which indicated he knew her. She may have said she didn't recognize the e-fit Sam had shown her, but Loveday knew it wasn't true. So why was she lying? What on earth could Marietta have to hide?

She got back to the cottage at the same moment Sam was leaving. 'Sorry, love, no time for breakfast. Have to make an early start.' He kissed her on the cheek, but she reached up and put her arms around his neck and kissed him full on the mouth.

Sam looked down, smiling. 'What did I do to deserve that?'

'I love you, that's what,' she said, touching his nose and laughing up at him. 'I'd also say have a good day, but I'm guessing you might not.'

'I'll settle for *you* having a good day. How about it?' Sam said.

'It's a start I suppose,' Loveday said. 'Keep in touch and let me know if you want to meet for lunch, or a drink, or anything.'

'I will, but don't hold your breath on that one,' he said as he got into the Lexus.

IT WAS HALF an hour later and only just beginning to get light as Loveday drove into Truro. She was trying to remember what was in her diary for that day, but the weekend and the run up to the wedding had thrown her slightly, not to mention what had happened to poor Rebecca Monteith. She had decided to push all thoughts of the murder from her mind as she walked into the editorial office later, but one look at Keri's face told her that was not going to be possible.

'It's all over the papers,' Keri said, lifting a copy of the *Morning News* and flapping it around. 'What on earth happened?'

Loveday took the paper and wrinkled her nose at the headline. *'Wedding guests quizzed as woman is murdered.'* She sank down on her chair. She knew Sam wouldn't be happy about this kind of coverage. Keri was still staring at her.

'Well? Are you going to tell me what happened?'

Loveday sighed. 'It's true, I'm afraid. Someone was killed in the hotel where the wedding reception was held. Fortunately Merrick and Connie had left for their honeymoon before the body was discovered. Hopefully they still won't know anything about it and that's the way I'd like it to stay.'

'So did she have anything to do with the wedding?' Keri said. 'I mean, would Merrick and Connie have known her?'

'I don't think the victim had anything to do with the wedding.'

'Do you know who she was? It doesn't say in the paper.'

Loveday hesitated. She knew Keri would recognize Rebecca's name as soon as she mentioned it. Should she tell her? It was going to come out anyway. She took a deep breath. 'The dead woman is Rebecca Monteith.' She waited as Keri frowned. She knew she was trying to recall why the name was so familiar to her. And then realization dawned. 'Rebecca Monteith, the artist?' Keri repeated, her eyes wide.

'Yes. But don't ask me any more about it because I don't know. I doubt if Sam knows any more either.'

Keri was clearly shocked. 'I know murders are horrible, but when it's someone you know it's so much worse.' She shook her head. 'Poor Rebecca.'

It had turned nine and people were beginning to drift into the office, nodding morning greetings to Keri and Loveday as they sat at their desks.

Loveday lowered her voice. 'I know what's happened to Rebecca is awful, but we have to put it out of our minds if we can. We have loads of work to do and even though it's not easy, we have to get on with it.'

'Yes, of course,' Keri said, pulling up the day's diary events on her screen. She glanced down the list of engagements. 'You have an appointment with the woman who runs her own jewellery business.' She looked across and Loveday nodded.

'Jan Sharp, yes I remember. What time was it arranged for?'

'Ten o'clock actually. Even if you leave now you'd be cutting it fine.'

'No, it's OK, I'll get there.' Loveday was already on her feet and gathering up her things. 'Can you ring her please, Keri, and tell her I'm on the way?'

'Consider it done,' Keri called after her as Loveday left the office.

THERE WAS something inherently sad about seaside resorts in the winter. They needed the warm carefree days of summer and holidaymakers jostling with each other along the seafront. They needed the packed beaches where excited children ran amok and parents kept a watchful eye from their deck chairs, parasols and windbreaks. Most of the holiday shops were closed as Loveday drove along the front. Jan had a unit in the arcade. It was one of only two that seemed to be open for business. Although what business they expected to do on a cold wintery morning in St Ives Loveday had no idea.

Jan Sharp was a young woman with a bubble cut of blonde hair, sea green eyes and a permanently startled expression. She also created some of the most beautiful silver jewellery Loveday had ever seen. They reminded her of the sea and sand and the wide blue skies of St Ives. She spent an hour with the woman, handling and admiring piece after piece of her work as she recorded her story.

'I stay open on the off chance that somebody will drop in and buy something.' She smiled at Loveday. 'But it's my workshop so I'm here anyway. It's no real hardship to have the place open to the public, even if there isn't any member of the public actually here.' When she smiled her emerald eyes lit up.

Loveday told her how beautiful her work was and took some pictures which she explained would be placed in a half-page feature. The young woman was delighted.

Loveday was in a more positive frame of mind when she left the jewellery workshop and began to stroll back to her car. She hadn't intended visiting her friend, Lawrence Kemp, but it felt like a while since she'd last seen him. She was trying to remember how long it had been. There had been that art exhibition in Penzance way back before Christmas, but they'd only had time for a brief drink together. She was looking forward to seeing him again. The place where he lived at the top of the hill overlooking St Ives Harbour had once been a herring store owned by a local fisherman. Lawrence now had the top floor of the building. The accommodation wasn't what Loveday would have described as homely, but it suited him. It was a place where he could work and he often said how much he appreciated the solitude it offered.

She climbed the stairs to his front door and gave a light tap. There wasn't any response so she knocked again, louder this time and the door opened. Lawrence's thin face broke into a wide grin when he saw who was standing there. 'Loveday! What the devil are you doing here?' He threw his arms wide and gave her a bear hug. 'How the hell are you?'

'I'm great.' She laughed, following him through a kitchen littered with the paraphernalia of painting activities. Art brushes were strewn across the table and the windowsill was lined with glass jars stained with messy colours. The kitchen led into the room Lawrence used as a studio.

The view from the window always made Loveday gasp. It looked directly over the bay. There was even a little balcony from where she knew Lawrence sometimes painted. But today the doors were firmly closed. Far below she could see a stiff breeze ruffling the surface of the dark water in the harbour.

There was an easel with a painting in progress in the middle of the room. A palette of colours lay on the floor beside it.

'Oh, Laurence I'm disturbing your work. You're obviously busy,' she said, nodding to the easel.

'I'm never too busy to see a dear friend.' He pulled a stool from under a trestle table and indicated for her to sit.

'So, what brings you to St Ives on a horrible February day?'

'Work, I'm afraid. I was interviewing a young woman down on the front about her jewellery business. We're going to do a nice feature about it in the magazine. She makes some beautiful stuff.'

Lawrence gave a smile of recognition. 'You must be talking about Jan.'

Loveday nodded.

'Yes, you're right she is extremely talented. She deserves to do well. I hope when the tourists come in a month or so she will do some decent business down there.'

He looked around him. 'I haven't offered you anything. Would you like a coffee?'

'Only if it's not any trouble,' Loveday said. She didn't mention her pledge to stop drinking coffee.

Lawrence had already disappeared into the kitchen and Loveday sat looking around her. He wasn't a man who favoured creature comforts, but she guessed his bohemian lifestyle was what he enjoyed. According to Sam, Lawrence was now selling his work online. At least that's what he'd told him when Sam called in to pick his brain about one of his cases recently. She screwed up her face. If Lawrence was making decent money he certainly wasn't spending it on himself.

He came back scratching his chin. 'This is really embarrassing, but I don't have any coffee. I forgot I needed to do a shop.'

'Never mind,' Loveday said brightly. 'I have a better idea. Why don't I buy you lunch at the pub?'

'Pub's a great idea.' Laurence gave her his wide grin. 'But lunch is on me otherwise I'm not coming.'

Loveday laughed and shook her head. 'OK, I give in. Lunch is on you. But I have to warn you, I'm absolutely ravenous.'

They strolled arm in arm down to the Sloop Inn, chatting about old times as they went. It suddenly occurred to Loveday that Lawrence may have known Rebecca Monteith. They were all part of the same artist world after all. And Cornwall was a very small place. She waited until they had found a table in the dark recesses of the pub and were checking the menu.

'I can recommend the fish pie,' Laurence said.

Loveday wondered if lunch at the Sloop Inn was a regular thing for him. He certainly didn't seem to be domesticated. She couldn't see him actually cooking a meal for himself, in fact she couldn't ever remember him having cooked for himself. But then they never had lived in each other's pockets.

'The fish pie sounds good,' she said. 'Can I have half a cider to go with it?'

Laurence stood up and gave a little bow. 'Whatever madam desires.'

Loveday watched as he ordered their food at the bar. He was still as thin as ever, but the ponytail had grown longer, and there were streaks of grey in the brown hair now.

'So, how are you and Sam doing?' he asked, returning with their drinks and squeezing into the tiny booth they had chosen. 'Are you two still living in your little matchbox in Marazion?'

'Next to Cassie and Adam, yes that's us. Our cottage may be a bit on the bijou side, but we love it. We would rattle around in it if the place was any bigger.'

'Ah well, to each his own,' Laurence said.

Loveday had no idea what he meant, but she smiled anyway and turned to him. 'Do you know a woman called Rebecca Monteith, Lawrence? She's an art expert from Penzance.'

'Rebecca?' He was thinking about that. 'Yeah, I think know Rebecca,' he said. 'What about her?'

Loveday put a hand to her temple, embarrassed. She hadn't really expected that response. 'I didn't realize you actually knew her, Lawrence. I'm sorry but it's bad news. Rebecca was killed at the weekend.'

He stared at her. 'Killed? You mean like in a road accident or something?'

'No. It was more shocking than that. She was murdered.'

Laurence shook his head. 'But that's terrible. I didn't know her well, but what I remember was good. She was a nice woman.'

'She would have been a similar age to you, Lawrence,' Loveday said.

His eyes were fixed on the far side of the pub and Loveday wondered if he'd heard her. He was clearly trying to recall things.

'She was part of the community here, I believe. I'm going back years, long before I came to Cornwall. But I've heard people talk about her. And of course she comes back here now and again.'

Loveday listened, waiting for him to go on.

'She was married to an artist.' He leaned in closer. 'Although the word is she was gay.'

'I didn't know she was gay,' Loveday said. 'Or that she'd been married.'

'Oh yes, there was a child too, I believe, but they split up and the baby went for adoption. At least that's the story going around at the time.'

Loveday watched his face crease into a frown. 'I'm trying to remember her husband's name.' He gazed around him and pointed to a painting on the far wall. 'That's him. He painted this?'

Loveday got up and went to inspect the painting. It was an image of surfers emerging from the sea, their skateboards making splashes of colour on the canvas. She peered at the name on the corner. 'I can't make out the name,' she called back to Lawrence. 'It looks like David something.'

Laurence snapped his fingers. 'David Gow. That's it. I remember now. He was quite talented at one time, but I think he stopped painting. I certainly haven't heard anything about him in years.'

Loveday came back to the table and got her mobile phone out. She googled the man's name, and a picture appeared on the tiny screen.

Lawrence leaned across her to look at the image on her phone. 'Yes, it's him. Ugly devil, isn't he?'

Loveday stared at her phone. This was the man Rebecca had been married to? The father of her child? The picture had clearly been taken some years earlier, but there could be no mistake. She was looking at the man Cadan Tremayne had been arguing with at the wedding reception.

CHAPTER 8

Bethany Farm Cottages, on the outskirts of Godolphin, were a neat little row of houses that Sam immediately identified as holiday lets. Wooden tubs filled with spring flowers sat by the front doors of three of the four properties. Sam glanced along the row, guessing the biggest one at the end was where Rebecca Monteith had lived.

As he and Will stood there the door of one of the houses opened and a harassed looking woman bustled out. She stopped, her eyes travelling suspiciously from one to the other. 'Can I help you?' The sharpness in her voice clearly telling them they had no right to be there.

Sam and Will produced their warrant cards and the woman examined each one in turn. She sniffed. 'You can't be too careful. We get all sorts down here.' She raised a plump hand to her face and pushed back strands of grey hair.

'Can we ask who you are?' Sam enquired.

'Lavinia Treacher. Call me Vinnie, everyone does. My husband Roderick and I run this place.'

'Caretakers or owners?' Will asked.

The woman looked at him as though he wasn't right in the head. 'We own the place of course.' She nodded to the end cottage. 'Apart from the far away one. Roderick sold it.' She looked as though she thought that had been a bad idea.

'Is that Rebecca Monteith's cottage?' Sam asked.

'Yes, it's hers. It would have been a holiday let like the others if I didn't have such a dim husband.' She shook her head. 'Oh, he's regretting it now all right, but then he never did take advice from me. The profit is in holiday rentals, not sales.'

'I don't suppose you have a key for it?' Sam said.

The woman looked askance. 'Course we don't have a key for it. Didn't you hear me? It belongs to Miss Monteith.'

'We need to have a look around the cottage,' Sam said, bestowing a patient smile on the ill-tempered woman. 'Can you help us?'

Vinnie Treacher scowled at them and then nodded towards the cottage. 'You see that bush to the left of the door?' Sam and Will nodded. 'Well, you could try there, she keeps a spare key buried in the leaves underneath the shrubbery.'

The woman turned to plod away when Sam called after her. 'Can I ask what you're doing here today?'

Vinnie Treacher wheeled back to them. 'Getting them ready for the visitors of course. They'll be here at Easter. We keep a high standard here. These properties are gleaming inside, which is why every one of them is rented out from the end of the month right through until October.'

Sam nodded. 'Where can we find you if we need to speak to you again?'

The woman pointed to a path leading through the trees. The farmhouse is up there. That's where Roderick and I will be. Although why you would need to speak to us I have no idea I'm sure.' She hesitated. 'Talk in the village is it was Miss Monteith as got herself murdered in the fancy hotel. Is that why you're here?'

'Thank you for your help, Mrs Treacher,' Sam said curtly. 'Like I said, we'll get back to you if we need to speak to you again.'

'I don't know why all you people need to come here. Can't you leave the poor woman in peace now that she's gone.'

Sam frowned, glancing at Will. 'What do you mean *all you people*? Has anyone else been here?'

'Only the other detective.'

'What other detective?' Sam stared at her. 'Can you describe him?'

The woman sighed. 'Don't you even know what each other are doing? He came here, exactly like you two, asking the same questions.'

'Did he go into the cottage?'

'Of course he did. Is that not what I'm saying?'

'Can you describe this other officer?' Will repeated Sam's question.

The woman thought for a minute. 'Untidy, short spiky hair dyed blond. His jeans were torn.'

Sam took the e-fit from his pocket. 'Is this him?'

The woman screwed up her face and nodded. 'I think so. Yes, it's him.'

Sam and Will eyed each other as the woman turned to leave. They made no attempt to stop her.

'What d'you make of that, boss? Victor Paton must have known we would come here. He was taking a risk turning up here. What d'you think he was after?'

'No idea,' Sam said, kicking aside the leaves under the shrubbery to find Rebecca's house key. 'Maybe there'll be a clue inside.'

The front door led straight into a small sitting room. They stepped in and looked around them. Only a trained professional would have realized the cottage had been searched. It appeared orderly enough, yet a few items were out of place. Sam's eyes travelled along the shelves of the bookcase. One book had been replaced upside down. The clock on the mantelpiece had not been centred and Sam noticed a drawer in a large bureau in the corner had not been properly closed.

Will shrugged. 'Wish we knew what he was looking for.'

'Your guess is as good as mine,' Sam said. 'But it is intriguing.'

'One thing's for sure.' Will's eyes were scanning the room. 'If it was Paton who was here before us, he wouldn't have left any fingerprints.'

'No,' Sam said slowly. 'He wouldn't be that careless.'

A painting above the fireplace had caught his attention and he moved forward for a closer look. It was signed Laura Knight. Even he had heard of Dame Laura Knight. He wondered if it was an original work. From what Loveday had told him about Rebecca he suspected that it probably was original. In which case it would be very valuable. So why was she leaving a spare key under a bush at her front door?

Will was still standing in the middle of the room contemplating his surroundings. 'This looks as I imagine a lecturer's room at university would be like,' he said, his eyes travelling over the vast collection of books and the artwork on the walls. 'All this stuff is quality. Look at some of these ornaments. They haven't come from any bargain basement.'

Sam headed for Rebecca's bedroom. Like the public room, it was neat and tidy, but not what Sam would have described as feminine. He picked up a small framed photograph from the bedside table. It was a photo of a baby. Everything about the picture suggested it was old. But whose baby was it? What child was so important to Rebecca that she would keep a picture of it by her bed?

Will had followed him into the bedroom and he handed him the photo frame. 'We'll take this back with us,' he instructed.

They returned to the sitting room with Sam looking

confused. 'Why would Rebecca Monteith book into an expensive hotel in Truro when she had this place?' He looked at Will.

The detective shrugged. 'I don't know, boss. I guess that's what we're here to find out.'

CHAPTER 9

The address they had for Marietta Olsen was a tiny mid-terrace house off Melville Road in Falmouth that had been divided into two flats. The number of students out and about as Sam negotiated the narrow streets was evidence of how close it was to the university.

'Marietta isn't here,' the woman who opened the door at flat number 29 said. 'Was she expecting you?'

The officers produced their ID. 'Perhaps you could tell us where we can find her?' Sam said.

The woman frowned. 'She'll be at college.'

His eyes narrowed. 'And you are?'

'I'm Elise Clark, Marietta's flatmate.' She looked up at him. 'There's nothing wrong, is there?'

'No, only routine enquiries. May we come in?'

If Will was surprised by Sam's request to step inside Marietta's place when she wasn't at home, he knew better than to show it.

'Routine enquiries about what?' the woman asked, leading them into a small cluttered sitting room.

Sam wasn't sure routine enquiries had been the right phrase.

He was more than curious to see the inside of this flat. It was nothing he could put his finger on, he just had a feeling something wasn't right here. Why had Marietta not told her flatmate about a murder that had happened at a wedding reception she had attended? It wasn't exactly a routine event.

The woman was still looking unsure. 'Marietta isn't in any trouble, is she?'

Sam smiled. 'It's nothing like that. We'd simply like a few words with you.'

Elise Clark stepped aside, clearly still unsure if she should even allow these people in.

'Do you both rent this property?' Sam asked.

'No, I own the place. Marietta is my tenant.'

'Ah.' Sam nodded. 'So not a flatmate then?'

'Well no, but it's hardly important, is it? We're friends.'

'But you are Marietta's landlady,' Sam said.

'Technically, yes. I suppose so. We don't think of it like that.'

'Did you know Marietta was a guest at a wedding this weekend?'

'I knew she was going to a wedding, yes.'

'She didn't tell you about the police investigation at the hotel where the reception was held?' He fixed her with an inquisitive stare, but the woman didn't flinch.

'I don't know anything about that. It was late when Marietta got home last night, and she was off to college first thing this morning. We've hardly spoken.'

Sam nodded. 'Do you have a job, Miss Clark?'

'I don't see what it has to do with anything.'

'Is there a problem?' Will asked.

'Well, no. I don't understand why you want to know.'

Will and Sam waited.

'I don't see what difference it makes,' Elise said with a shrug. 'I work in a bar downtown.'

'Does this bar have a name?' Sam said. The woman was testing his patience.

'The Brush and Pen. It's on The Moor.'

Sam recognized the pub name. It was too bohemian for his taste, but it suited the artists who hung out there. He had a sudden thought. 'Does Marietta work there?'

'She does the odd shift. I put in a word for her. It's not a regular thing, merely pin money for her.'

'Pin money?' Sam repeated. 'I thought all students were poor.'

Elise glanced away. 'Not Marietta. Her family has money.'

Sam had followed Will's gaze to a painting on the wall. 'Is this her work?'

'No, I painted that.'

Sam went to take a closer look. It was a street scene in Falmouth that captured the busy tourist aspect of the town. He was no art connoisseur but even his eye could spot the work was amateurish. He turned to face her. 'You didn't fancy joining Marietta at art school?'

'Not all of us can afford such luxury.' It was a throwaway response, but it caused Sam to wonder if Elise was jealous of her tenant.

He nodded to Will, who pulled the e-fit of Victor Paton from his jacket pocket. 'Do you recognize this man, Miss Clark?'

Elise glanced at the image and then quickly away. 'No. Who is he?'

'Take another look, please. Are you sure you don't recognize him?'

Elise slid her gaze back to the e-fit. 'I don't recognize him.'

'OK. Thank you for your help.'

'Should I tell Marietta you called?' Elise said as the officers turned to leave.

Sam smiled. 'That won't be necessary. We'll contact Miss Olsen ourselves.'

'What was that all about, boss? Why do you think she was being so evasive?' Will asked as they walked back to the car.

'Not sure,' Sam said. 'But something is going on there. If those two are such good friends, then why didn't Marietta tell her about the murder?'

'Maybe it's like she said. If Marietta really didn't get back until late last night they probably didn't have time to talk.'

'It doesn't stack up, Will. Rebecca Monteith's murder has been all over the news, not to mention the papers.'

'So, you think she was lying?'

'I do.'

'What about the e-fit? Did she really not recognise the man?'

'I think our Elise is an accomplished liar. The question is, why? Is she looking out for Marietta, or is it herself she's protecting? Either way, I'd bet my pension that she's on to Marietta right now warning her to expect a visit.'

The Falmouth School of Art was only five minutes away. The middle-aged, balding man behind the reception desk looked up at them and lowered his spectacles. 'Can I help you?'

'We're here to see one of your students. Marietta Olsen?' Sam told him as he scanned their ID cards. The man strained his neck to look around them in an attempt to catch a glimpse through the glass doors. Sam followed his nod to a bright yellow C5 car leaving the car park. 'That's her,' he said. 'Sorry. If you'd been a minute earlier, you would have caught her.' He pushed his spectacles back up his nose. 'Can anyone else help?'

'No, it's fine. It wasn't anything urgent,' Sam said, exchanging a look with Will. Was it a coincidence the girl had left minutes before their arrival, or had Elise already been busy on her mobile?

LOVEDAY WAS HAVING difficulty imagining the elegant, silver-haired Rebecca Monteith as a hippy artist living amongst the St Ives community. But then the times Lawrence had referred to must have been about twenty years ago and times had changed. Rebecca had undoubtedly changed. Why wouldn't she have fallen for the penniless David Gow? But having a child by him, that was a different thing.

She was approaching the Chiverton Roundabout and turned down past the industrial units into Truro, her mind still going over what Lawrence had said. Maybe she should have contacted Sam from the Sloop Inn? She knew how important this new information about Rebecca might be. She'd hesitated because she couldn't bear putting that last memory of Tessa into his head again. The Sloop Inn was the last place Tessa had been before her untimely death. She'd been having an evening out in the pub with a friend and had died when a drunk driver collided with her car on the way home. According to Will, who had taken Sam to the hospital that night, he'd been devastated.

Even now, Loveday imagined she sometimes caught a look of sadness about him. She knew he still thought of Tessa. No, she decided. She couldn't have contacted him from the Sloop Inn. He had only recently come to terms with the news his first wife, Victoria, was to marry again. He was fine with that but hated the idea the new man might replace him in the affections of his children, Jack and Maddie.

'You have a visitor,' Keri called out to Loveday as she walked into the office. 'She's waiting downstairs.'

'Who is it?'

Keri shrugged. 'She refused to give her name, but she's been driving the girls down at front counter mad with her pacing around this past half hour.'

Loveday slipped out of her coat, dropping it on her chair. She didn't need any more mysteries, but her curiosity was getting the better of her. 'I suppose I better find out what she wants.'

The young woman pacing the floor in reception was trendily dressed in a long brown suede coat. She spun round at Loveday's approach. It was Marietta Olsen!

'Sorry for bursting into your office like this but you said I could contact you.' Her words poured out in a defensive tumble.

Loveday led her to the leather-covered bench seat in the corner. 'Sit down, Marietta. Now what's all this about?'

'Why do the police want to speak to me?'

Loveday frowned. 'Do they?'

Marietta gave a nervous nod. 'Your detective friend Mr Kitto. He came looking for me with one of his colleagues this morning.'

Loveday put up a hand. She knew Sam had questions for the girl, but she didn't want to lie to her. 'I expect it was a routine enquiry. The police must speak to lots of people when they investigate such a serious crime.'

Marietta gave her an unsure look. 'I'm not a suspect then?'

'Why would you ask that? Do you know something about the murder?'

Marietta Olsen glanced away and Loveday saw the fear in her eyes. She caught the girl's hands, forcing her to look at her. 'Tell me what's wrong,' she said, softening her voice. 'What is it you're afraid of?'

Marietta bit her lip. 'It was the picture Mr Kitto had. I recognized the man.'

Loveday blinked. 'You mean the e-fit Detective Inspector Kitto showed you at Edward Tremayne's house?'

The girl nodded. 'He was in the hotel that day. He's been stalking me.'

'Oh, for heaven's sake, Marietta! Why didn't you tell Sam about this?'

Marietta jumped to her feet. 'I shouldn't have come. Please forget everything I've said. I…I made a mistake.'

She turned, heading for the door, but Loveday caught her

arm. 'Don't run off, Marietta. We can talk about this. Everything will be fine. Sam and I will help you.'

Marietta's eyes were bright with tears. 'It's Cadan,' she said. 'I think he's mixed up in this.'

Loveday's heart sank. Cadan! Merrick's half-brother had got into so many scrapes over the years and Merrick invariably bailed him out. What had he been up to now? If he'd done something to bring more grief to his family she would kill him herself.

She sighed. 'What's Cadan done this time?'

Marietta hesitated, clearly unsure how much she should say.

'Tell me, Marietta. What has Cadan done?'

'I'm not sure.' The girl bit her lip. 'He lied to Sam as well when he said he hadn't recognized the e-fit picture. He knows the man. I've seen them speaking together. So, you can see why I can't talk to the police.'

Loveday shook her head. This wasn't what she wanted to hear. 'I'd say it's even more important you now speak to them. Tell me, why do you believe this man has been stalking you?'

Marietta took a deep breath. 'I've seen him. He follows me around. He's been there outside the house and at the college.'

Loveday's brow wrinkled as she tried to work out what was going on. Had Cadan employed Victor Paton to investigate Marietta? But why would he? Or maybe he had spotted the private eye tailing his girlfriend and had been warning him off when Marietta had spotted them talking?

Another thought struck her. Perhaps it was Cadan the man has been following? Loveday thought that would make more sense. Cadan involved himself with some shady people. It wasn't so far-fetched that one of them was having him investigated by a private eye.

'Look,' she said gently. 'Come upstairs with me. I'll make us some coffee and call Sam. He'll know best what to do.'

'No!' Marietta shouted, jumping up and heading for the door. 'I told you. No police!'

'Wait, Marietta,' Loveday pleaded. 'Don't leave. Have you mentioned this to Cadan?'

Marietta shook her head. 'You don't understand. I can't let Cadan think I don't trust him.'

'Why not?' Loveday said.

Marietta fixed her with a stare from startled blue eyes. 'Because I love him, of course.'

'I TOTALLY LET HER DOWN,' Loveday later told Sam. 'She came to me for help and I went and made things worse.' He had suggested they meet for a drink in the Crab and Creel, explaining he was unlikely to be home before midnight that night.

'Advising Marietta to go to the police is hardly letting her down,' Sam said. 'She should have listened to you.'

Loveday ran a finger around the rim of her wine glass. 'What about Cadan? What do you think he's up to?'

'I've no idea,' Sam said. 'But you can be sure I'll find out.'

'There's something else you should know about Cadan.'

Sam's eyes narrowed. 'Go on.'

Loveday took a sip of her wine, trying to work out the best way of explaining what she had to say. She put her glass down. 'I called in on Lawrence when I was in St Ives this morning.'

'Yes?'

She could hear the apprehension in his voice.

'He told me Rebecca Monteith was known in St Ives in the old days. She was part of the artist community. The thing is, Sam, she was married and apparently they had a child.'

Sam's head flicked up. He was staring at her. 'What else did Lawrence tell you?'

'He said he thought the child had been adopted, at any rate Rebecca didn't bring it up.'

She watched Sam empty his beer glass. 'There's more,' she

said. 'I googled Rebecca's ex-husband on my phone and guess what?'

'Tell me.'

'He was one of the waiters at Merrick and Connie's wedding reception. But that's not all. I recognized the man.' She swallowed. 'I saw him having an argument with someone at the do.' She looked up. 'It was Cadan.'

CHAPTER 10

Sam was already on his way to the hotel to question the waiter David Gow. Loveday's discovery that he had been Rebecca's husband could be a major breakthrough for them. His mobile phone rang as he arrived at the hotel car park. 'Yes, Amanda?'

'I'm at Trevere Manor, sir. We've found somebody here who recognizes the e-fit.'

'I've just pulled into the car park,' Sam said. 'I'll meet you in the reception.'

'Yes, sir, I'll wait right here.'

He smiled at the excitement in her voice. Amanda obviously felt this was something she could get her teeth into. Sam knew he should give her more responsibility on the team. She was better than only being trusted to handle the admin stuff. He wished she had a less aggressive attitude when interviewing witnesses.

There was no sign of his young detective constable as he walked into the hotel, but Sam recognized the young woman Jackie Bissett behind the reception desk as the member of staff they had talked to before.

'I think your colleague is somewhere around, Inspector. I can get someone to fetch her for you if you like.'

'No need, I'm right here,' Amanda said, appearing beside them from a back corridor. The young woman with her was about twenty years old. She was looking distinctly nervous.

'This is Melanie Pendle, sir. She's one of the chambermaids here. She thinks she saw a man go into Rebecca Monteith's room on the morning of the wedding.'

Sam glanced to the young woman behind the reception desk. 'Is there anywhere more private we can go?'

Jackie Bissett nodded. 'You could use the manager's room. It's over here. He isn't around at the moment, so you have it all to yourselves.'

'Thank you,' Sam said, as the three of them followed her into Frederick Manning's, office. 'Take a seat, please, Miss Pendle,' he said, smiling at the young woman.

She sat down, looking from one to the other.

' tell Inspector Kitto what you told me, Melanie,' Amanda said.

'I only saw him for a minute, so I can't be absolutely certain.' She swallowed. 'But it did look like the picture you showed me.' She nodded to Amanda.

'Can you show Melanie the e-fit again please, DC Fox' Sam said.

Amanda produced it.

'You think this is the man you saw?' Sam said. 'Now take your time, have a good look at him.'

Melanie stared at the image and nodded. 'That's him, I'm sure it is. It's him or somebody very like him.'

'And what exactly was he doing when you saw him?' Sam asked.

'He was going into a bedroom. The one where the lady...' She bit her lip.

'What time was this?' Sam asked.

'About midday.'

'Can you tell us what you were doing in the corridor?'

'The bridal couple had booked a room. Sometimes wedding parties do that. They like maybe to tidy up before they go off on their honeymoon. Or even to have a little time to themselves before going back to join their guests.'

Sam nodded encouragingly.

The girl continued. 'I was taking some fresh towels into the room for them. That's when I saw him come out of room 215.'

'You didn't see him go into the room?' Sam asked.

Melanie shook her head.

'Do you think the man saw you?' Amanda cut in.

'Well, he would have been blind not to have seen me. He almost knocked me over as he rushed past.'

'You didn't go into room 215 yourself?' Sam said.

The chambermaid's eyes widened as she stared at him. 'Of course I didn't.'

'Were you in the room at all while this particular guest was occupying it?' Sam asked.

She shook her head. 'The guest had left word with reception that she didn't want to be disturbed.'

Sam looked at Amanda. 'Really? Who told you that?'

The young woman looked flustered. 'I might have made a mistake there. Maybe it was a *"Do Not Disturb"* notice on her door.'

'Well, which one was it?'

'The notice, I think. I'm sure I saw it there at one point and then it must have been removed.'

Sam pursed his lips, not sure how relevant this new piece of information was. He would need to think about it.

'Are you aware of any other visitors that guest might have had during her stay here?' The question came from Amanda.

Melanie shook her head. 'I only clean the bedrooms. I don't know anything about who visits who.'

Sam smiled at her. 'Do you know if any other members of

staff recognized the e-fit? Sometimes things are not obvious at first and it's only when you have time to think about it that you realize you may actually have seen someone.'

'No,' the woman said. 'I've spoken to some of the others in the kitchen and no one else saw this man, well so they're saying.'

'OK,' Sam said. 'Thank you for your time, Melanie. If we need to see you again we will contact you.' Sam was thinking as he watched the young woman leave the room. If the face on their e-fit really was Victor Paton, of the Falmouth Detective Agency, and he knew he had been seen visiting Rebecca Monteith on the morning she was murdered, it was no surprise he had disappeared.

Sam quickly briefed Amanda about what he knew about the waiter David Gow and watched her eyes round like saucers as he said he had been Rebecca's husband.

'And he works here at the hotel?' she said.

'Seems so.' He was thinking of Cadan Tremayne and Loveday telling him she'd seen the two men arguing. He hoped Merrick's half-brother was not involved in this. But it was looking likely he knew more than he had told them.

'I'm going to find David Gow,' he told Amanda. 'Keep this room free for us and I'll try to bring him back here.' She nodded, watching him as he left the room.

Jackie Bissett was tapping into her computer behind the reception desk as Sam arrived. 'I understand you have a waiter here by the name of David Gow?'

Jackie looked up. 'Gowie? Yes, he works here. Why do you want to speak to him?'

He stopped himself from frowning at her. 'Can you tell me if he is on duty today?'

'He's not actually.'

'Do you have any idea where I could find him?'

'You could try the staff chalets behind the hotel. Gowie has one of them.' She gave him a worried look. 'He's not in any trouble, is he?'

Sam wondered why she was so concerned. 'It's only an informal chat.'

David Gow opened the door at Sam's first knock and looked curiously at him. 'You're the detective,' he said. 'What do you want with me?'

'I think you know the answer to that. May I come in?'

The man moved aside and Sam stepped into the small cabin. It was tidy, but basic. No creature comforts here. It reminded Sam of the upstairs downstairs practices where wealthy Victorian households forced domestic staff to live in cramped attic rooms while the family themselves enjoyed spacious luxury below.

David Gow was following Sam's gaze around the room. 'Is not much, but it's a bed. It can be quite expensive finding accommodation in Truro and I don't earn much as a waiter here.'

'No, I think it's fine,' Sam said. 'Can we sit down for a moment?'

Sam watched the man fidget as he waited for the questions to come. He launched straight into it. 'You were married to Rebecca Monteith?'

David Gow wrapped his arms about himself. 'It was a very long time ago. Things are different now…the world is different.'

'Do you mind telling me what went wrong between you?'

'I would if I knew. I was head over heels in love with Becky. I thought she felt the same. We were both a bit hippy back then, the artist community in St Ives was like that.' He shrugged, remembering. 'I was only mildly talented. It was Becky who was the talented one. And then one morning I woke up and she wasn't beside me. It was some time before I found the note.' He swallowed and Sam thought he detected a wetness in the man's sad brown eyes. 'She said she loved me, but it wasn't enough for her. Cornwall was suffocating, she said and she had to get away.'

'And yet she came back,' Sam said.

David Gow shrugged his thin shoulders. 'I'd no idea she was here in Cornwall.'

Sam folded his arms. 'I have this problem you see, David. I'm wondering why your ex-wife would come here to stay at this hotel – the hotel where you work – when she has a perfectly good house not so very far away. Can you explain why she would do that?'

'I have no idea,' David Gow repeated. 'But it certainly wasn't to find me.'

'That note you've described Rebecca having left you. Was it the last you heard from her?'

'No. I had a letter about a year later saying she wanted a divorce. It was someone else who told me she'd had a child. In some ways hearing that was more hurtful than when she left me. We had made a child together and she didn't tell me.'

'How do you know it was your child?'

'I challenged her and she admitted it. I made it a condition of my agreeing to the divorce that she should tell the truth, but she refused to say if it had been a boy or girl. She would only admit she'd had the child adopted.' The man's shoulders slumped.

'I'm very sorry,' Sam said. 'That must have been hard.' He couldn't imagine how terrible it must have been to have your child wrenched from you.

'It's all water under the bridge now.'

Sam paused, watching him. 'How could you not know your ex-wife was staying at the hotel?'

'The only contact I have with guests is when they come into the dining room – and Rebecca didn't.'

'So who would have served her in her room?' Sam said.

'Any of the waiting staff could have been asked to do that, yes, including me. But it never happened.'

Sam was inclined to believe him. He knew he could check

which staff members delivered meals and snacks to Rebecca's room.

'As for her staying here, well, I repeat, I have no answer, but I certainly didn't know she was a guest. None of the staff here even know I was married, let alone that I have a child somewhere in the world.'

'Don't you ever wonder what happened to the child?' Sam couldn't imagine the pain of having no contact with his children, but if he had never known them then perhaps he would feel differently.

'I can't afford to wonder what became of the child. That part of my life has gone.'

'Does that include your painting?' Sam looked around the room. There was no indication an artist lived here.

'I don't paint any more,' he said quietly.

'You were on duty for the wedding reception on Saturday?'

The man nodded. 'You must know I was. I was interviewed by your people same as the rest of the staff and I'll tell you what I told them. I neither saw nor heard anything unusual.'

'What about having a confrontation with one of the guests? You didn't mention that.'

David Gow gave him a cross stare. 'I don't have confrontations with hotel guests. It would be more than my job's worth.'

'Maybe confrontation was too strong a word. What about argument?' Sam met the man's stare. He was suddenly not looking so confident.

'I don't know what you mean.'

Sam sighed. 'You were seen having an argument with a wedding guest.'

'I don't think so.'

'I'm talking about Cadan Tremayne, Mr Gow.' Sam held up a warning finger. 'And before you try making any more denials, the witness is 100% reliable. I want to know how you know this man.'

David Gow got wearily to his feet and went to the window to stand with his back to Sam. 'I used to work behind the bar in a casino in Bristol.' He was talking so quietly that Sam had to strain to catch the words. 'Tremayne was a regular there and we used to chat when the place was quiet. He's good at wheedling information out of people.'

Sam pressed his mouth into a hard line and kept his eyes on the back of the man's head. He knew exactly what he meant. Cadan made a living from knowing other people's secrets.

'One night a customer who'd had a big win on the tables had gone to cash in his chips. He was so engrossed in stuffing the notes into his pockets that he didn't see me coming with my tray. He turned and collided with me. The tray flew out of my hand along with all the glasses on it.

The man blamed me of course, yelling for everyone to hear about how clumsy I was. I was furious.' He shook his head. 'You would have thought winning all that cash he would have been happy, but the big win meant nothing to him. He still treated everyone, especially the staff, like we had all crept out from under a stone.'

He turned and came back to perch on the edge of the camp bed. 'If it had been anyone else I wouldn't have done it. I would have handed the note back, but this character deserved to be taught a lesson.'

'What note would you have handed back?' Sam asked.

'The guy dropped a handful of bank notes as he was stuffing them in his jacket pocket. He had been so busy blaming me he didn't even notice them fluttering to the floor.' He slid Sam a guilty look. 'OK, I know I should have handed them back, but he'd made me so mad. I scooped the notes under the tray as I picked up the broken glass. Another member of staff had come over with a cloth and we tidied up the mess together.'

Sam frowned. 'What does all this have to do with Cadan Tremayne?'

'He saw the whole thing, including me taking the money. I assumed at first he would report me. I couldn't afford to lose that job. But he didn't report me, he did worse than that. He blackmailed me.'

'How blackmailed? What did he want in return for his silence?'

'Information,' David Gow said flatly. 'He knew the kind of things bar staff heard as they served drinks. And he was right. I did catch snippets of conversation between customers drinking at the bar. Until then I had kept it all to myself. It was their business, their secrets. But now Cadan Tremayne was telling me if I wanted to keep my job then I had to pass on what he called the juicy bits. He even had me hovering around customers eavesdropping on their conversations.' He looked away. 'I wasn't proud of myself.'

'I still don't see what all this has to do with your argument with him at the wedding reception.'

David frowned. 'It was about Cadan thinking he could continue to blackmail me, but I'm done with all that. Back in Bristol he was bullying me, but I eventually found a new job in another part of the city and left the casino. If Cadan Tremayne couldn't find me then he had no hold over me. I was earning less money in this new job, but I didn't mind. I had got my life back. All that was a year ago, and then I got this job.'

He looked at Sam. 'Cadan recognized me on Saturday and took me aside thinking he could take up where he'd left off back in Bristol. He said the manager was a friend of his and threatened to tell him about my background at the casino unless I did what he asked. But I was wise to him this time. I told him if he tried to do that then I would let everyone know how he had blackmailed me. He had as much to lose as me if it was made public.'

'And that was why you were arguing?'

David nodded. 'Cadan isn't used to people standing up to him, but he could see I meant what I said and he wasn't happy.'

'No,' Sam said, getting to his feet. 'I don't imagine he was.'

He found Amanda still waiting for him in the manager's office, scrolling through her phone. Someone had brought her a cup of coffee and she was looking quite at home. She jumped up when Sam entered the room. 'Everything all right, sir? Was the victim's husband any help?'

Sam quickly appraised her of his conversation with the waiter, leaving out what the man had told him about Cadan. He needed to speak to Merrick's half-brother before going any further with that.

The post mortem report was on his desk when he got back to the station and he flicked through it. It didn't contain any startlingly new information. Rebecca Monteith had died from a stab wound to the heart. The weapon would have been a knife with possibly a seven-inch blade. Sam shook his head. If they had the knife it might help progress things. But they didn't. He looked out over the incident room. Will was at his desk and he beckoned him in. 'Any more news from the Penzance Museum?'

'Not a lot,' Will said. 'As soon as it was confirmed she had worked there, DC Carter and DC Rowe went along to speak to the staff. According to Malcolm Carter's report, everybody liked her. She knew her subject and was a respected member of staff.'

'Was she still employed as the museum's archivist?' Sam asked.

'That's right,' Will said. 'Our lads had a good nose around the room where she worked but there didn't seem to be any personal stuff in there.'

'I think we need to pay the museum another visit,' Sam said, checking his watch. It was getting late and his team was still working. 'Send everyone home, Will. You go too. We'll need everybody back here bright and early in the morning.'

Sam sank back on his chair. The pile of paperwork in his inbox had grown since he'd looked through it that morning. The thing seemed to have a life of its own. No matter how much time he spent attending to the admin stuff, his tray never seemed to empty. He reached for the top sheet and settled to making a start on the paperwork. An hour later he decided he was making little progress and was about to call it day when his eye fell on the stack of folders on his desk. The murder wasn't the team's only case.

He pulled the folders across to him and started to check through them. One case in particular caught his attention. There had been an attempted break-in at the Penzance Museum the previous week. He stared at the report. Why had no one flagged this up? He read on. A small window at the rear of the property had been broken. The intruders had apparently thought they could reach in and undo the latch, but they hadn't reckoned on the level of security there. The museum was home to many priceless artefacts. It also housed a collection of paintings and sketches by some of Cornwall's most celebrated artists.

Sam scanned through the report again. No access had been gained to the premises, but the museum people had been understandably concerned. He flicked through the papers and found another related report. The incident was significant enough to have involved a forensic team. They'd taken an impression of a footprint found by the broken window and made a cast. Sam was staring at a picture of the cast. It had been estimated to have been made by a size 10 trainer. He shook his head and sat back. Everyone wore trainers these days. However, it was another reason to go back to the museum and speak to staff again.

CHAPTER 11

Giselle Olsen kicked off her fashionable slippers and crossed the elegant drawing room to answer the telephone. She listened, frowning a little as she tried to make sense of the caller's words. And then her eyes flew open and her hand clutched at her throat. Someone was playing a hoax on her. An evil hoax.

'I'm not listening to this. I'm going to put the phone down,' she cried. The call had shaken her.

'If you hang up on me you will never see your daughter again. Think about it. Be sensible.'

'I don't understand. What do you want? Why are you doing this?'

'I've told you, Mrs Olsen. We have your daughter. If you don't co-operate then your daughter will die.'

'Who are you?' Giselle snapped. 'What nonsense is this? Our daughter is at college in Cornwall.'

'Ah, but she's not. She's with us now. Would you like to hear her?'

A wave of nausea swept through Giselle's body as she heard

her daughter's frantic cries. 'Help me…somebody help me.' She could hear Marietta sobbing. 'They're going to kill me!'

Giselle was struggling to speak. What kind of horror had she stepped into? 'Who are you?' she asked again, her voice trembling.

'I told you, Mrs Olsen. You're not paying attention. We're the ones who have your daughter. Are you listening now?'

Giselle nodded helplessly at the phone. 'I'm listening.'

'That's good, very good. What we need you to do now is to contact your bank and make immediate arrangements to withdraw £500,000 from your account. Then tomorrow, when you've done it, you and your husband must drive to Cornwall. You must book into Bartons Hotel in Truro and await further instructions. One more thing, Mrs Olsen. No police. Do you understand? No police or your daughter dies!'

'What? No! This can't be happening.' Giselle's heart was pounding. She felt a rush of panic. She reached for the bureau to steady herself. 'Where is my daughter? What are you doing with her?'

'I'm losing patience, Mrs Olsen.' The voice was sharp. 'I told you. We have your daughter. We will return her when you deliver the half million. If you contact the police you will never see her again. It's all quite simple.'

The sound of the caller ending the call buzzed in Giselle's ear. 'No,' she yelled at the dead phone line. 'Please don't go!' Her breath was coming in pants. But the caller had gone. Her hand shook as she put the phone down. She was wringing her hands, pacing the room. What should she do? She had to speak to Nils, he would know what to do.

NILS OLSEN STRAIGHTENED his tie and put on the jacket of his expensive dark suit. He pressed the button on the intercom that connected him with his secretary in the outer office. 'You can finish off and go home now, Yasmin. I'm about to leave myself.'

'Thank you, sir,' Yasmin said. 'See you in the morning.'

Nils was making a final check of his computer screen when his mobile pinged. He lifted it. 'Giselle. I haven't forgotten our dinner guests, I'm…'

'Nils!' Giselle was sobbing. 'It's Marietta! She's been taken!'

'What? Try to stay calm, my love. You're not making any sense. Who's taken Marietta?'

'I don't know,' Giselle whimpered. 'They phoned now. They've got her, Nils. They've got Marietta. I heard her on the phone. I heard Marietta. She's terrified. We have to do something.'

'I'm coming right home,' Nils said.

Giselle flew into her husband's arms as he rushed into the room twenty minutes later. 'Calm down, my darling,' he said, stroking her hair. ' tell me what's happened.' He spoke soothingly, trying to control the turmoil inside him as he listened to his wife relate the conversation with their daughter's kidnapper.

Her voice was trembling. 'They want £500,000 or they will kill Marietta.'

'We have to contact the police,' Nils said. 'We can't deal with this on our own.'

'No!' Giselle grabbed his arm, her eyes wild. 'Didn't you hear me? They said they would kill Marietta if we do that.'

Nils stood up and moved around the room, his head in his hands. He swung round to her. 'What are you saying? That we should hand over half a million pounds to these people? How do we know the whole thing isn't an evil hoax?'

'I heard her, Nils. I heard Marietta. They played me a recording.' Her voice broke as she stared at him. 'She was pleading for her life.' She put her hand on her husband's arm. 'We have no choice, my love. We have to trust these people.'

Nils raised his eyes to the ceiling. 'I don't even know if we can raise so much cash, not in the time frame they are insisting on.'

'We have to try, Nils.'

He nodded. 'I'll start making calls now. I wish I'd been here when the call came through.' He paused. 'I don't suppose you recognized the voice?'

'No, I couldn't even tell if it was a man or a woman. The voice was distorted.' She looked at her husband. 'People will notice if Marietta has disappeared. Cadan will certainly be worried. What if he calls the police? The kidnappers said no police.'

'We have to get our story right then. We must tell people Marietta has gone to relatives in Sweden.'

'But how do we explain her sudden disappearance. She wouldn't go away without telling Cadan where she was going.'

'We could say she'd been having a difficult time personally and needed to be by herself for a while. We could tell anyone who asks that Marietta has gone to a retreat in Sweden. At least that would keep the police off our backs.'

'Yes, yes, it might work,' Giselle said distractedly.

'What about tonight's dinner party?' Nils asked. 'Have you contacted the Delaneys and cancelled?'

'I did that while I was waiting for you to get home. I told them you were under the weather. I'm not sure they believed me, but anyway, they're not coming.'

CHAPTER 12

*L*oveday didn't recognize the number, but she gave her mobile number to many people so it was hardly surprising she'd get calls from unfamiliar numbers. What did take her aback when she answered the call was the voice she heard.

'Cadan!' Her mind immediately flashed to Edward. Had he taken ill in the night? He'd looked so frail last time she'd seen him. But Cadan wasn't calling about his father.

'It's Marietta,' he said.

She could hear the anxiety in his voice. Loveday balanced the phone between her shoulder and her ear as she saved the work on her screen.

'OK, Cadan. Calm down. What's happened to Marietta?'

There was a split second of silence and she thought he was taking a deep breath.

'She's disappeared,' he said.

'What do you mean, disappeared? I saw her yesterday.'

'We were supposed to meet up in Falmouth yesterday after she'd finished her classes for the day, but she didn't turn up. I waited an hour or so.' He paused. 'Marietta has never had any concept of time. She's often late, so I wasn't that bothered. But when it got to around 7 o'clock and she still hadn't appeared I got really pissed off.' Loveday heard him draw a breath. 'OK, so I went on a pub crawl,' he said. 'There's plenty of pubs around Falmouth Harbour, but I wasn't fussy.'

'Didn't you try ringing her?'

'What? Well of course I did. Her mobile was going on to answer phone. I even went to her digs, but she wasn't there and the place was in darkness.'

' because Marietta stood you up, Cadan, doesn't mean she's disappeared.'

She could hear his irritated sigh at the other end of the call.

'People don't stand me up,' he snapped. 'But I was good and mad, which is why I was back at her digs first thing this morning. I wanted to have it out with her.' There was another moment's silence. 'She wasn't there,' he said.

'You mean there was no reply to your knock?'

'No, I mean she wasn't there. Her flatmate said she hadn't seen her since she left for college the previous morning. She'd assumed Marietta and I were together as she quite often stayed over with me at Morvah.'

Loveday's mind went back to the conversation with Edward Tremayne at Merrick and Connie's wedding, and his obvious disapproval that Marietta and Cadan were sleeping together. Maybe the girl had simply come to her senses and dumped Cadan. Loveday pursed her lips, thinking. But it didn't explain why she had disappeared.

'I don't want to go to the police, not yet,' Cadan said. 'Can you help me to find her, Loveday? You said she came to see you yesterday. What was that about?'

Loveday had some thinking to do before she was ready to share any details of it with him. 'This isn't something we should be discussing on the phone, Cadan. Where are you?'

'In that wine bar at the top of Lemon Street.'

'I know it,' she said, glancing at her watch. It was 12.30. She hadn't made any arrangement to meet Sam for lunch. 'Stay put and I'll join you there.'

Keri had already left the office for a dental appointment. Loveday thought about leaving her a note to say where she'd gone but decided against it. She went out of the building and walked quickly up the wet street to meet Cadan. He was sitting at the bar staring morosely into an untouched glass of red wine. 'That won't get Marietta back,' Loveday said, settling into the empty seat next to him.

Cadan slid the glass across to her. 'You have it then.'

A barman appeared, looking unsure whether to ask if she wanted to order something. Loveday nodded to a corner table. 'Can you bring a couple of coffees? We'll be over there.'

The man smiled. 'No problem,' he said.

Cadan frowned, but he allowed Loveday to lead him away from the bar. They settled themselves in the corner table and she studied his unshaven face. She suspected he'd slept in his clothes. He looked seriously hung-over. This wasn't the crass, confident Cadan she knew. Would he be in a state like this if his girlfriend had dumped him? Did Marietta mean that much to him? She wondered what he hadn't told her.

The coffees arrived. 'Drink it,' Loveday said. 'You look like you haven't slept.'

Cadan pulled a face. 'I've been out looking for Marietta.'

'So, tell me again what happened – from the beginning.'

Cadan rubbed his hands over his face and pushed his fingers through his hair, which made him appear even more dishevelled. 'It's like I told you. Marietta has disappeared.'

'You said you went to her flat this morning?'

Cadan nodded. 'That's right. She stays with a woman called, Elise. I don't know her second name. She said she hadn't been bothered about Marietta not appearing last night because she thought she was with me.'

'And when you told her she hadn't been with you? How did she react?'

'She looked worried. She said I should contact her parents.'

'And did you?'

He nodded. 'Elise more or less insisted on it. She took me inside and found a number for them. I told them I probably already had their number on my phone somewhere. The Olsens and I go way back. They run a marketing company in Bristol and I've had business dealings with them.' He looked up, his eyes glazed. 'That's how I met Marietta. I'm not sure her parents were happy about our relationship, but that was their problem. It had nothing to do with them.'

'So, what did Mr and Mrs Olsen tell you?'

'It was Marietta's father, Nils Olsen, I spoke to. He said his daughter had gone off to a retreat in Sweden. He said she didn't want to be contacted, she needed some time on her own.'

Loveday frowned. 'And you didn't believe it?'

'Of course not. Marietta would never go off without at least telling me where she was going.'

'But why would they lie?'

'I have no idea, I only know something is going on here and I'm worried about Marietta.'

Loveday blew out her cheeks and sat back. 'I don't see how I can help, Cadan. If her parents say she's perfectly well I can't believe they would lie. I don't know what else to say.'

Cadan's face crumpled into a frown. 'I thought you might have an idea where Marietta had gone.' He narrowed his eyes at her. 'You said she came to see you yesterday. What was that about?'

'She was looking for advice. She thought someone was following her.' Loveday paused, watching him. 'Sam showed you a police e-fit of the man. You said you didn't recognize him.'

Cadan shook his head, a little too vigorously, she thought. 'No, no I don't know who that was.'

'We need to bring Sam into this, Cadan. In fact, I'm going to ring him right now.' She had expected an objection, a desperate bid to dissuade her from making that call, but none came. Cadan hung his head and gave a defeated nod.

Sam picked up on the first ring. 'Where are you, Sam?' Loveday asked.

'Will and I are on our way to Falmouth.'

'To see Marietta?'

'Why are you asking?' Loveday could imagine Sam frowning at the phone.

'I'm with Cadan,' she said quickly.

'Cadan? I don't understand. What are you doing with Cadan?'

Loveday took a breath. 'I think you should have a word with him, Sam. He's worried about Marietta.' She paused. 'He says she's disappeared.'

'Where are you?'

'At the moment we're in a wine bar in Lemon Street, but we can meet you back at the magazine office.'

'Can we make it the station?' Sam asked.

She could tell how seriously he was taking this. 'Yes, of course,' she said.

Cadan's expensive sports car was parked in the street, but Loveday didn't think he was in any state to drive. 'We'll take my car,' she said. He already had his car keys in his hand and flashed her a cross look. For a moment she thought she would have a tussle on her hands dissuading him from driving, but he gave a resigned shrug and stuffed his keys back into his pocket.

SAM HAD RUNG AHEAD to tell the sergeant at the front desk to expect Loveday and Cadan and to put into an interview room until he and Will arrived. The detectives made their way to the room as soon as they got there. Sam nodded to Loveday and raised an eyebrow Cadan's dishevelled state. Knowing how much importance Merrick's half-brother put on his appearance he was clearly in a bad place.

Sam and Will pulled out chairs and sat down. 'OK, Cadan,' Sam said, eyeing the man. 'Would you like to tell us what this is all about?'

'Marietta's gone. I don't know where she is. She's not at her flat and she's not answering her phone.' The words were fired out in short, breathless sentences.

'Try to stay calm, Cadan,' Sam said gently. He wasn't sure what was going on, or even if he believed the man. Honesty wasn't one of Cadan Tremayne's best qualities. 'When was the last time you saw her?' he asked.

Cadan's brow furrowed as he tried to remember. 'Sunday evening. She was supposed to stay over with me at Morvah but changed her mind and drove back to Falmouth. She said she had preparations to make for college next morning. I obviously wasn't happy about that.' He sucked in his bottom lip. 'We had a bit of a row. I wasn't used to her standing up to me.'

'Sounds like this is about a row between the two of you.' Sam tilted his head and narrowed his eyes at him. 'Why are you pushing the panic button, Cadan? What is it you're not telling us?'

Cadan's movement as he lunged at Sam was so violent his chair skidded across the floor. Loveday jumped to her feet, grabbing the man's collar and yanking him back. 'Sit down, Cadan,' she ordered as Will retrieved the chair and set it back on its legs. 'Sit down now or Sam will throw you out of here.'

Sam hid a smile. 'Thank you, Loveday. I think we've got this.' He saw

Loveday colour.

'Do you think I'm making this up?' Cadan hissed at him. 'This is not about Marietta and I having a row. How many times do I have to tell you? She's disappeared and I'm at my wit's end with worry.'

Sam held back on his response, allowing the silence to fill the room. He'd not seen Cadan behaving like this before. It was in complete opposition to his normal snide comments and arrogance. But at least he was looking a bit calmer.

'There's a place on The Moor, in Falmouth where artists hang out. They have a live music session on Monday nights. Marietta and I always call in there. I texted her that we should meet there as usual.' He pulled a face. 'She didn't turn up. She wasn't answering her phone. When her flatmate told me this morning that Marietta hadn't slept there last night I began to get really worried. I contacted Loveday. I didn't know what else to do.'

Sam nodded, not taking his eyes off the man. 'Why did you deny recognizing the e-fit I showed you on Sunday? Now is not the time for secrets, Cadan. You must tell us what you know.'

Cadan moved the tip of his tongue across his dry lips. He sighed. 'Marietta said the man in your e-fit was stalking her. I didn't take it seriously. I told her she was imagining things.' He fixed Sam with a worried stare. 'But she wasn't imaging it, was she? That man has kidnapped her.'

'D'YOU THINK Tremayne is right, boss?' Will asked, turning to Sam as they drove to Falmouth later. 'Has Victor Paton abducted the girl?'

'I'm not sure what's going on. Hopefully we'll know more when we've spoken to the woman she shares with.'

Will screwed up his face. 'There's something not right about this,' he said as they pulled up in front of the terrace of houses where Marietta lived. The door was opened to them before Will had even knocked.

'Inspector! I hope Mr Tremayne hasn't been pestering you about Marietta.' Elise Clark's small hazel eyes darted from one to the other. She had scraped her brown hair back into a ponytail so severely it gave her a startled look.

'Pestering us?' Sam repeated as they followed her into the small front room. 'Why would you say that, Miss Clark?'

'Because of Marietta, of course. Her boyfriend was here this morning in a terrible state saying she was missing. I suggested the best people to speak to were Marietta's parents, so I invited him in and we called them together.' She gave an exasperated sigh. 'They told him Marietta was fine and that she's taken herself off to a retreat for a few days. I was relieved to hear it, but not Cadan. He refused to believe she'd gone off somewhere without telling him.'

'So, you're quite satisfied all is well?' Sam smiled at her.

'I am now, yes.'

'But you didn't discover this until this morning? Weren't you worried yourself when Marietta didn't come back last night?'

'No, I thought she was with Cadan. When I realized she wasn't I was sick with worry until Cadan called her parents.'

'Have you any idea why Marietta would suddenly decide to go to a retreat?' Sam asked.

'No. Well...I'm not sure.'

'If you know anything, you must tell us,' Will cut in.

Elise turned away from them, her head in her hands. She began pacing the room. 'This is all my fault. I should have said something at the time. I wanted to go to the police, but Marietta insisted I stay out of it.'

'Stay out of what?' Will asked.

'Marietta was being watched, Inspector. I saw the man outside the flat a couple of times. It was creepy to see him lurking in the shadows.'

'What does this have to do with Marietta?' Sam said.

'Didn't I say? I saw him following her. I watched him waiting out there until she'd got into that funny little car of hers. I saw the man jumping into another car and driving after her.'

She spun round to stare at Sam. 'I was sick with worry that night. I tried to ring Marietta on her mobile, but she wouldn't pick up when she was driving. When I did eventually catch up with her I told her she was being followed and said she should go to the police. She told me I was imagining things and not to be so silly. But I kept an eye on her after that. The man was still hanging around the terrace and I could see Marietta was scared.'

'So why didn't *you* report it?' Will asked.

Elise gave a hopeless shrug. 'You're right. I should have ignored her when she told me to mind my own business.' Her eyes locked with Sam's. 'It's my fault that Marietta has gone off, isn't it?'

'I'm sure you did what you thought was right,' Sam said. 'If Marietta gets in touch, you must call us.'

She nodded. 'Of course.'

Will glanced back at the flat as they drove off. 'None of this makes any sense. Could the Olsens be lying? Could they be following a kidnapper's instructions? But it doesn't feel right either. When the whole of Cornwall and beyond is looking for Paton why would he do something like this? He must be aware there's no way he'll be escaping under the radar. He knows it's only a matter of time before we find him. I can't see him kidnapping someone.'

'Well, according to Elise, and what Marietta herself told Loveday, the man was definitely stalking her.'

'Or keeping her under surveillance,' Will suggested. 'Maybe he was being paid to keep an eye on the girl. And maybe it's the person who was paying him to watch her that's abducted her.'

'Maybe,' Sam said thoughtfully. 'We need to redouble our efforts to find him. And I definitely need to speak to the Olsens.'

CHAPTER 13

The Tremayne family's temporary housekeeper made no attempt to hide her surprise as Cadan marched into the house with Loveday by his side.

She was carrying a tray of tea things and followed them into the big sitting room where Edward sat by the fire. He looked up. 'Loveday! How nice. Come over here where it's warm. You look half frozen.'

Loveday rubbed her hands together and smiled at Edward as she went to the fire.

'Put the tray down and leave us, please,' Cadan said to Molly.

'He means "Thank you, Molly",' Edward said, glaring at his son.

'I know what he meant,' Molly said, depositing the tray on the low table beside Edward, and turning on her heel she left the room.

Loveday and Cadan had agreed on the drive to Morvah not to worry Edward by mentioning Marietta's disappearance, but judging by the way the old man was looking at his son, Loveday felt they might have to rethink that.

'You look like a tramp, Cadan. What's got into you?' His

glance moved to Loveday. 'I suppose you had to bring him home because he wasn't fit to drive himself.'

Loveday swallowed. 'It wasn't exactly like that, Edward.'

The old man was staring at his son. 'Perhaps you would like to explain exactly what it was like.'

Cadan sucked in his bottom lip and raised his eyes to the ceiling. 'Marietta is missing, Father. I've been out all night trying to find her.'

Edward's shoulders stiffened. 'Missing? How can she be missing? I don't understand.'

'What Cadan means is Marietta didn't go back to her room in Falmouth last night,' Loveday interrupted, lowering her brow at Cadan. 'He's spoken to her parents and they insist she has gone to a retreat in Sweden for a few days.'

'Sweden? Why Sweden?' Edward asked.

'Exactly!' Cadan sprang forward. 'My father gets it. Even if she has gone to a retreat…why Sweden?'

'Isn't that where her parents hail from?' Loveday suggested.

'Her father's Swedish, her mother is French,' Cadan fired back. 'But Marietta has no connection with Sweden. She has no family there anymore. They're all dead.'

Edward shook his head. Loveday could see his son's outburst had unsettled him.

'Have you told the police?' he asked.

'Sam knows all about it,' Cadan said.

'And we can be assured he'll be doing all he can to find Marietta,' Loveday said. She turned to Cadan. 'Why don't you go up and have a shower and maybe try to catch a few hours' sleep. You look all in.'

Cadan gave an exhausted shrug. 'I'll take the shower and get Molly to make me a sandwich, but I want to get back out there looking for Marietta.'

'I can wait and give you a lift back to your car,' Loveday offered. 'You should be fine to drive by then.'

'No need. I'll call a taxi.' He turned, heading for the door. 'And thanks for your help,' he called over his shoulder as he left the room.

It was getting dark as Loveday drove back through the city traffic to the office. Sam had told her he was going to Falmouth to talk to Marietta's flatmate again. According to what he later told Cadan, the woman had believed the Olsens' story that their daughter had taken herself off to a retreat. She couldn't give the police any more helpful information, so it seemed Sam hadn't discovered anything new. In her head Loveday went over the previous day's conversation with Marietta. The girl had certainly been worried about her stalker. Was Cadan right in his conviction that the man had abducted Marietta? Would there soon be a ransom demand – or could something completely different be going on here? She needed to write all this down to make sense of it.

When Loveday got back to the office her colleagues were beginning to pack up for the day. Keri gave her a relieved look. 'I was about to call out the cavalry. Where have you been, Loveday? I thought we'd agreed you wouldn't go off the radar like this again.'

Loveday gave an apologetic smile, raising her hands in a gesture of surrender. 'Sorry. I've just realized my phone has been out of charge. Were you trying to call me?'

'Only a hundred times. You don't exactly steer clear of trouble. I saw you and Cadan Tremayne taking off from the car park and thought there might be a problem.'

'There is,' Loveday said, throwing down her bag and pulling out her chair. 'But not for me. Cadan's says his girlfriend has disappeared.'

'Disappeared, or dumped him?' Keri said.

Loveday gave a resigned shrug. 'That was my first thought,

but I think there's more to it now. Sam is certainly taking it seriously.'

'Really? What does he think happened to her?'

'Her parents seem very clear that Marietta has gone off to a retreat, but Cadan doesn't believe that and I have to admit it doesn't sound right. He's been trying to phone them.'

All around them colleagues were leaving their desks and calling their 'good nights'.

'You should go too, Keri,' Loveday said, switching on her computer. 'I have a few more things to finish off here.'

Her PA gave her a concerned look. 'I don't like you staying in the building on your own at night.'

Loveday gave her an amused frown. 'When did you turn into my mother?'

Keri started counting off reasons on her fingers. 'When you go off for half the day without checking in with the office…When I see you driving away with the boss's brother – the most notorious con man in Cornwall…When you don't answer your phone for hours…When you have this history of getting yourself into life-threatening situations?' She raised an eyebrow. 'Should I go on?'

Loveday sighed. Keri was right. There had been more than one occasion when she'd got herself dangerously entangled in Sam's murder investigations and almost lost her life in the process. She was lucky she had friends like Keri to watch out for her. 'You're right,' she conceded. 'It was irresponsible of me not to check my phone. I should have let you know where I was.'

'Yes, you should have,' Keri said, unable to stop her mouth quirking into a smile.

Loveday reached across the desk and touched her friend's arm. 'It won't happen again, Keri. I promise.'

Keri shook her head, still smiling. 'Why do I find that so hard to believe?' she said as she left the office.

But Keri's words were still running through Loveday's mind

as she ran down the back stairs to the staff car park more than an hour later. The security light came on showing her beloved Clio was the only vehicle there. She had no reason to suspect she was being watched, but she picked up her step anyway as she crossed to the comfort of her car. Loveday plugged in her phone to charge it before driving off. It registered numerous missed calls from Keri and two from Sam. She sighed. No doubt he would also be reading the Riot Act to her for being out of touch. She rang him and put the phone on 'hands free' as she left the car park.

'Hi, Sam.' She was deliberately trying to sound cheerful, 'Sorry I missed your calls. You've caught me heading home.'

'I might be there before you then,' he said. 'Shall I get a takeaway?'

'Never mind that. What's happening about Marietta?'

Sam described his and Will's visit to interview Elise Clark, the girl's flatmate in Falmouth.

'So not much help there then?' Loveday said. 'Poor Cadan. Have you heard any more from him?'

She could hear Sam sigh at the other end of the phone. 'He's been calling regularly, but there's nothing we can tell him.'

'So, what happens now?'

'It all depends on whether or not I manage to track down the Olsens.'

'You're not thinking they're deliberately staying out of your way?' Loveday said.

'Well, where are they? I might have to send one of the team up to Bristol to find them. In the meantime, we need to take this very seriously. I've already set up a coastal search with the assistance of the coastguards. We should get helicopters up at first light tomorrow. Teams of volunteers and other agencies will search the moorland and other remote areas.'

'I really don't like the sound of this, Sam.'

'It's routine when we get a report of a missing person. I know her parents have told Cadan she's not missing, but they haven't provided any evidence to back this up. And now they to seem to have disappeared.' He paused. 'I still have a feeling Victor Paton is the key to everything that's happened.'

The idea that had been running through Loveday's head was so unlikely she was reluctant to mention it. But as far as she could see, the police had nothing else to go on. 'I don't suppose you're anywhere near Falmouth, Sam?'

'I'm almost there actually. I wanted to check up on the surveillance team that's watching Paton's detective agency before getting home. Why?' She could hear the suspicion in his voice.

'I have an idea. Will you bear with me on this?'

'Go on.'

'Falmouth's only half an hour away from me. Could we meet up there?'

'I'm not sure why I'm agreeing to this, but I suppose we could.'

'Great. I'll see you in the seafront car park.'

The closer Loveday got to Falmouth the less confident she felt about her idea, but she had involved Sam now and she could hardly back out. He was already in the car park when she arrived and she pulled the Clio alongside his Lexus. He came around and held his arms out to her, planting a kiss on her forehead. He tipped up her chin so she was looking into his eyes. 'Care to tell me what all this cloak and dagger stuff is about?' He grinned down at her and she suddenly felt embarrassed.

'I've probably got this all wrong, but now we're here you might as well hear me out,' she said. Loveday led Sam across the car park to the boundary rail and pointed out to the backs of the Church Street shops. 'Where exactly is your surveillance team positioned, Sam?'

'They're installed in a store room above one of the shops opposite the entrance to the Falmouth Detective Agency. If our man had come anywhere near the place they would have spotted him.'

'Not if there was a way in at the back of the building,' Loveday said.

'There isn't. We checked.'

'OK,' Loveday said, standing beside him, her hand on the car park rail. 'Tell me what you see.'

'Considering it's pitch black out there, not much,' Sam said.

'OK, what can you hear then?'

Sam listened. 'Nothing.'

'Listen again,' Loveday said. 'There is a sound out there. What is it?'

Sam cocked his head. 'Only the clink of the boats at their moorings.'

'Exactly,' Loveday said. 'Boats! What if Mr Detective Agency had a boat and was able to get into the back of his premises using that? He was a DS at the Met after all. I don't expect he's stupid. He'll know exactly how you've set up your surveillance.'

She looked up at Sam's profile in the dark and could make out that he was biting his lip. 'When did your people last actually go into the property?' she asked.

'Wait here,' Sam instructed as he took off at speed across the car park and up into the street in the direction of his surveillance team. She could hear him barking into his phone for the officers to come down and meet him.

'What's happening, boss?' the shorter, heavier of the two officers he'd called asked as he and his colleague came running to meet Sam at the corner of the deserted street.

'We need to get inside that flat,' Sam said.

'But Victor Paton isn't there. We would have seen him,' the second man said. 'There's no way he could have got past us.'

'Humour me,' Sam said stiffly. 'But we're doing this gently. If our man is inside I don't want him scarpering.'

'He'll have to get past us first,' the stocky detective said.

'Not if he has an escape route at the back,' Sam said, as the three of them crossed the road and made their way quietly to the entrance to the Falmouth Detective Agency.

The tall detective forced the lock and Sam was relieved to see it wasn't alarmed. Victor Paton was clearly not worried about break-ins, but Sam suspected he probably had nothing of value to steal. As they approached the door to the agency they could hear a TV playing quietly. Sam put up a hand, warning the two officers to be silent. He swallowed and put his shoulder to the door. There was a loud crack and the door crashed open as the three officers rushed into the room. The man in the armchair froze for a split second before taking off across the room, but the tall detective sprang at him and caught his legs in a flying tackle. His colleague yanked the man's arms back and cuffed him.

Sam waited until Victor Paton had stopped struggling and they'd got him to his feet. His smile was cold. 'Good evening, Mr Paton,' he said. 'We've been looking forward to meeting you.'

CHAPTER 14

There were very few people about in Church Street, but those who were stopped to stare as the handcuffed man was marched to the detectives' waiting car.

Loveday stepped forward as Sam approached, unable to contain her excitement. 'You got him?'

He nodded. 'Thanks to you we did.' He flashed her a grin. 'But don't you go getting big-headed.'

'Who me?' She blinked, giving him an innocent stare.

'There's no sign of Marietta in there, but I've called out the forensic team, so if she's been in Paton's place they'll find the evidence.'

Loveday was thoughtful as she chewed her bottom lip. 'Are we thinking he could have Marietta hidden away somewhere?'

'*We* are not thinking anything. You are not part of this investigation, Loveday.'

She ignored the remark. Over his shoulder she could see the two detectives put Victor Paton into the back seat of their pool car. The stocky one got in beside him and the other started the car. They gave Sam a wave as they passed. Loveday thought they looked pretty pleased with themselves.

'I'm guessing you're not coming home,' she said, looking up at him.

'Sorry, I have to be here when the others arrive and then it's back to the station. We have to interview Paton as soon as possible.'

Loveday was beginning to feel optimistic as she left Falmouth and headed for home. If Cadan had been right and this man had abducted Marietta then surely he would admit it and tell them where to find her.

VICTOR PATON HAD BEEN in a cell at Truro Police Station for more than an hour when Sam arrived and ordered him to be put into an interview room. He called for the two arresting officers to join him. Sam knew the heavily built one was DS Jake McAuley and his surveillance colleague was DC Mark Owen. They had been seconded from another team when extra manpower had been needed. Sam was pleased with the job they did that night. They deserved to sit in on the interview.

DS McAuley took his seat beside Sam and set up the recording equipment while the other officer stood in the corner, arms folded.

Victor Paton had regained his composure and fixed Sam with an arrogant stare. 'Would someone mind telling me what I'm doing here?'

Sam eyed him. The man was an ex-detective. He would know all the police interview techniques. They would have to take this carefully.

'How long have you been a private dick, Mr Paton?'

Paton raised an eyebrow. 'Why?'

'If you are going to question everything I put to you we are going to be here for a very long time so I'll ask again, how long have you been a private eye?'

Paton blew out his cheeks and rolled his eyes. 'I set up the Falmouth Detective Agency two years ago.'

'How's business?' Sam asked.

'It pays the rent.'

'What are you working on at the moment?'

'Sorry, Inspector, can't say.' He smiled. 'Client confidentiality and all that.'

Sam slid the e-fit Loveday had helped construct across to him. 'Recognize yourself?'

Victor Paton glanced at it and shrugged. 'This could be anybody. What's it got to do with me?'

'I'd say it was a pretty good likeness,' Sam said. He narrowed his eyes. 'What were you doing at the Trevere Manor Hotel on Saturday?'

'I wasn't there.'

'We have two witnesses who will identify you.'

'Then your witnesses would be wrong, I told you, I wasn't there.'

'Do you know Marietta Olsen?'

'Never heard of her.'

'But you were seen loitering outside her flat,' Sam said.

'When was this?'

Sam flicked through the pages of his folder. He knew Cadan had been hazy about the dates he'd seen the man. He tried a shot in the dark.

'Wednesday, February 11th at 8 o'clock.'

A smile spread across Paton's face. 'I was interviewing a client in St Ives that night. Check my appointment book. I can give you a name and address if you like.' He folded his arms and the side of his mouth lifted in a sneer. 'So you can see, there's no way I could have been in Falmouth at the same time.'

'Who said anything about Falmouth, Mr Paton?'

A second of panic flashed across the man's cold blue eyes. 'You did.'

'No, I don't think so,' Sam said, his eyes never leaving the man's face. 'Perhaps you could share with us how you knew Marietta Olsen lived in Falmouth?' He sat back, aware that DS McAuley next to him had slid him a triumphant look. Sam kept his attention on Paton, watching him shift uncomfortably in his chair.

The silence filled the room, but Sam was in no hurry. He waited, still watching the man until he saw him swallow. He knew Paton was playing for time as he desperately tried to find a believable reason why he would know where the girl lived. Sam knew there could be none.

Paton shot a look from one officer to the other. He put up his hands. 'OK, so I was keeping an eye on her for a client.'

'What client? Why?' Sam fired at him.

'Can't say,' Paton spat back.

Sam knew it was only a matter of time now before the whole story came out. The man was a former DS. He would know there was nowhere for him to go. He had to tell them the truth.

'Where is Marietta?' Sam asked.

'How should I know? Tucked up in her bed in Falmouth probably.'

'She's not,' Sam said. 'Marietta Olsen is missing. But then you'll know all about it, Mr Paton.'

The man's surprise looked genuine. He frowned. 'How would I know?'

'Did you kidnap Marietta Olsen?' Sam asked.

'What?' Paton was out of his chair. 'What's this about? Of course I didn't kidnap her. Why would I want to do that?'

'For a ransom?'

Paton was shaking his head in disbelief. 'This is ridiculous. I know nothing about this. I'll admit I was keeping the girl under surveillance, but I didn't kidnap her.' His voice rose as he ran his hands over his spiky blond hair.

'Why were you keeping her under surveillance?' Sam persisted.

Paton blew out his cheeks again, his eyes darting around the room. 'I want a solicitor,' he said.

'Yes, of course, that's your right,' Sam said. 'But why would you need a solicitor if you have nothing to hide? tell us who your client is.'

Victor Paton threw up his hands. 'OK, I'll tell you.' He squared his shoulders and looked Sam directly in the eye. 'What I'm about to say is the truth. You know I'm a private eye. This is what I do. I follow people on the instruction of clients. I find things out about people for money.' He sucked in his breath and looked away. 'My client was Rebecca Monteith,' he said.

Sam's heart gave a lurch. It was a possibility that had run through his head when the chambermaid at the hotel had recognized the e-fit and said she'd seen the man leave the murdered woman's room. Were they about to tie up the case?

He deliberately took his time. 'So you admit our witnesses were right? You were in the Trevere Manor Hotel on Saturday, February 14th?'

Victor Paton nodded. 'Rebecca had asked me to report to her there. She gave me her room number and told me to go straight up there. She didn't want me asking for her at the hotel reception.' He paused, passing his tongue over his dry lips. 'I knocked on the door. There was no response. I waited a few seconds and tried the handle. The door opened and I went in. I didn't see her at first and thought she must be in the en suite, but the bathroom door was open and she wasn't there.' Another pause. 'That's when I saw her. She was lying in a pool of blood on the floor on the far side of the bed. I've seen enough scenes like this to know she had been stabbed. All I could think of was getting myself out of there. So that's what I did. I ran.'

Sam frowned. 'Aren't you a former police officer, Victor?'

'What's that got to do with it?'

'Well, I would have thought you would have reported what you'd found and stayed at the scene to help us.'

Victor Paton gave a disbelieving laugh. 'Like you would have believed me?' He shook his head. 'I could see you pinning this on me. I know how these things work and private eyes don't have the best of reputations.'

Sam ignored the comment. 'Tell us why Rebecca Monteith employed you.'

'She wanted to find her daughter. At least she wanted me to get evidence Marietta Olsen was her daughter. So yes, I had been following the girl. But I didn't kidnap her. If she is missing I know nothing about it.'

Sam didn't like the man, and he had already shown he was more than willing to lie to them, but he had a feeling this time he was telling the truth. Sam didn't believe he was involved in Marietta's disappearance.

The clock came into his line of vision and he was surprised to see it was after midnight. 'It's late,' Sam said. 'We'll continue this interview in the morning.'

'Does that mean I'm free to go?'

He smiled at the man. 'You know it doesn't. I'm sure we can find a nice comfy bed in one of our cells for you.'

SAM WAS HALF EXPECTING Loveday to be sitting up waiting for him when he got back to Marazion, but the cottage was in darkness and she was fast asleep in bed, her long dark hair spread out across the pillow. The sight filled him with an overwhelming tenderness. She looked so vulnerable lying there. He undressed quietly and slipped in beside her. She sighed softly as he slipped his arms around her. He was fast asleep almost before his head touched the pillow.

IT WAS STILL dark as Sam sat at the kitchen table later that morning, a piece of toast halfway to his mouth. He looked up as Loveday came in breathlessly after her jog. 'Only you, Loveday would go jogging in the dark on a freezing wintery morning.'

'Nonsense,' she said. 'It's invigorating.' Her face was glowing. She raised her hands in an enquiring gesture. 'Well? Have you found Marietta?'

Sam shook his head. 'Paton claims to know nothing about her disappearance and I think I believe him.'

Loveday sank onto a chair. 'So we're no further forward?'

'Not quite,' he said, standing up. 'I'll tell you the rest once you've had your shower.' He crossed to the sink to fill the kettle again.

Loveday was back in ten minutes, showered and dressed in work-smart charcoal slacks and cherry red sweater. 'So tell me,' she said impatiently as Sam poured tea into the mug he'd set out for her.

She stared at him wide-eyed as he described the previous night's interview with Victor Paton. 'So Marietta is Rebecca's daughter?' Her voice rose in disbelief.

Sam nodded. 'According to Paton it's what Rebecca thought.'

'So this is the child Lawrence mentioned. The one Rebecca had with her artist husband?'

'We don't know that. We have many more questions for Victor Paton when we interview him again today.'

Loveday was thoughtful. 'I take it he doesn't deny being in Trevere Manor during Merrick and Connie's wedding reception?'

'Oh, he was there all right, by appointment, according to him. He says he was there to rendezvous with Rebecca and pass on the results of his surveillance of Marietta.' He paused, staring grimly across the room. 'He took off after finding Rebecca's body in the hotel room and has been lying low at his flat in Falmouth, coming and going by boat from the back of the property after dark.' He raised his eyes to Loveday. 'Exactly as you suggested.'

'Was he able to confirm that Marietta was Rebecca's daughter?'

'That's one of the things we need to talk to him about today.'

Loveday put down her mug of tea. 'That's so sad. Poor Rebecca. She could have been on the brink of being reunited with her daughter.' She looked at Sam. 'Do you think that's why she was killed?'

'We have no idea.'

'Could Rebecca have paid someone to kidnap Marietta?'

Sam raised his eyes to the ceiling. 'You have a journalist's imagination, Loveday. I don't think for minute that's what's happened.'

Loveday took another thoughtful sip of tea. 'I wonder if Marietta found out about Rebecca being her mother?' She put up a hand to silence Sam's objection. 'If she was her mother I mean. I know it's not been proved yet. But supposing it's true and Marietta knew.' She shrugged. 'Perhaps she's run off rather than facing her real mother.'

'Why would she do that?' Sam frowned at her.

'I don't know.' She wrapped her hands around her warm mug. 'Marietta's parents are quite well off. Cadan told me they run a high-profile marketing agency in Bristol. He knows them. That's how he met Marietta.'

'What's your point, Loveday?'

'Well, she doesn't want for anything. I understand Mama and Papa Olsen pay her college fees and support her living in Falmouth. I was wondering what Marietta would do if she thought this new mother would take her away from the Olsens. Maybe she was worried she might lose her easy life and simply took off?'

Sam laughed, heading for his coat hanging behind the kitchen door. 'You should write fiction, Loveday. You're good at it.'

'Does that mean you don't like my theory?' she said, getting up and following him to the door.

'It's not a theory, my darling. It's a fairy tale.' He bent down to kiss her before going out to his car.

Loveday watched the tail lights of the Lexus move up the drive and disappear as the car turned right onto the seafront. She knew her suggestion was far-fetched, but something had happened to Marietta and the police could leave no stone unturned until they found her.

Her head was still full of thoughts about Rebecca and Marietta as she drove to Truro half an hour later. She wondered how Rebecca had managed to track the girl down in the first place. She tried to envisage Rebecca's circumstances when she discovered she was pregnant. She had left her husband and was possibly trying to earn a living as an artist. A child would have been a complication. Did she consider having a termination? Loveday couldn't see the woman she'd known ever doing that. Anyway, they knew she had put her baby up for adoption. She frowned as she sat in the queue waiting to access the roundabout. Did they know Marietta had been officially adopted? She wondered if Sam's team had checked that out.

Her mobile rang and she put it on hands free. 'Is this a bad time?' It was Cassie.

'I'm sitting in traffic, Cassie. Carry on.'

'I was wondering, are you free for lunch today? I have a meeting in Truro this morning, but we could meet in that nice little bistro in River Street. They do a wonderful lunchtime menu if you fancy it. How about 12.30?'

'Sounds great,' Loveday said. 'I'll look forward to it.'

CHAPTER 15

Cassie's choice of restaurant was the kind of place where you'd have no chance of getting a table unless you'd booked. It also looked expensive. Loveday spotted her at a corner table and waved as she made her way through the buzz of other diners.

'Are we celebrating something?' she asked, looking around her as she sat down.

'We certainly are,' Cassie said, her eyes sparkling.

Loveday raised an eyebrow. 'Well, don't keep me waiting.'

'I've signed a contract to refurbish *six* yachts for a boatyard in Falmouth.'

'That's wonderful, Cassie.' Loveday was catching her friend's excitement. 'Tell me more.'

'I knew this particular yard sold a lot of second-hand yachts because they do trade-in deals with clients who buy new boats from them. And since I run a business refurbishing yacht interiors it was a no-brainer to approach them and offer my services.'

'Will you have to take on more people?' Loveday asked.

'Probably.' Cassie picked up the menu. 'But I'm spoiled for

choice there so that's no problem.' She beckoned a waiter and asked for a bottle of Veuve Devienne.

Loveday gave her an amused look.

'Don't worry,' Cassie said. 'It's only sparkling wine, but I'm in the mood for something fizzy today. Now what are we having to start?'

Loveday stared at the menu. 'What's calamari?'

'Lightly spiced crispy fried squid with a garlic sauce. It's delicious,' Cassie said.

Loveday wrinkled her nose. 'Squid? I definitely won't be having that.'

Cassie laughed. ' have the brioche et champignons then. For the uninitiated it's mushrooms on toast.'

'That will do nicely, thank you,' Loveday said, running her eye down the list of main courses as their wine arrived.

Her French wasn't fluent, but she was able to make out that pave de steak was pan-fried Scottish pasture fed twenty-one day aged seven oz rump steak in a roasted garlic and brandy butter sauce with pommes frites.

'I'll have this,' she said, pointing, as the waiter took their order.

'Me too.' Cassie smiled up at him. He had filled their glasses and they raised them in a toast as he left.

'Now tell me,' Cassie said, lowering her voice. 'Has Sam solved his murder yet?'

'Cassie!' Loveday hissed, shooting a look around them and hoping none of the other diners had overheard the comment. 'It's not Sam's murder.'

'You know what I mean. Has he caught his man yet?'

'Not yet.' Loveday sighed. She realized Cassie knew nothing about Marietta's disappearance. 'But there was a development yesterday.' She corrected herself. 'No that's not the right phrase. It could have nothing to do with the murder.'

'I'm intrigued now,' Cassie said, her gaze widening.

'Cadan came to see me yesterday,' Loveday began. 'It seems his girlfriend, Marietta, has disappeared.'

'The lovely young girl who was with him at the wedding?' Cassie frowned. 'I don't like the sound of that.'

'No, it's worrying. Poor Cadan is frantic.'

Cassie's eyes never left Loveday's face as she described her part in Victor Paton's arrest the previous night. She wasn't sure how much of what Sam had told her she should be sharing with her friend. She decided on the minimum. 'The man denies any involvement in Marietta's disappearance. I think Sam believes him.'

Their food arrived and they ate through two courses in companionable silence.

'Shall we be completely decadent and have a sweet?' Cassie said.

Loveday sat back patting her stomach and shaking her head laughing. Her mobile phone rang and she fished it out of her bag. 'It's Priddy,' she said. 'She doesn't ring unless it's something urgent.'

Cassie sat up, listening.

'Hi, Priddy. Is everything all right?'

'Not really,' Priddy said. 'It's Jago's mother! She's been stolen!'

'OUR PRIORITY IS to find Marietta Olsen safe and well and preferably before the day is out,' Sam told his team of detectives as they gathered round him. 'The police and Air-Sea Rescue should already have resumed their search of the coast. Once we make this public we should have no trouble rounding up volunteers for a search.' He scanned the faces around him and allocated two detectives to co-ordinate a search of the moors. He turned to Amanda. 'Any luck yet with Marietta's parents?'

She nodded. 'We got some local plods to go knocking on their door. It appears they were in all the time, just not answering their phone.'

'So you've spoken to them?' Sam asked.

Amanda checked her notebook. 'They're still claiming Marietta is in Sweden but they are driving down from Bristol today, which is odd. I mean if they know where their daughter is, then why are they coming to Cornwall?'

'Exactly,' Sam said. 'We need to keep an eye on them. Can I leave it to you to look after them, Amanda?'

She nodded. 'Yes, sir.'

'You will all know by now that we arrested Victor Paton last night.' Sam glanced to the two detectives who made the arrest. Everyone nodded their approval. 'Paton claims to know nothing about Marietta's disappearance,' he said.

'Did you believe him, sir?' DC Malcolm Carter asked.

Sam sighed. 'We're not ruling him out, but yes, I was inclined to believe him. The forensic team that examined his flat certainly didn't find any traces of Marietta.'

'Did he admit to being at Trevere Manor on Saturday?' Malcolm chipped in again.

'He did eventually,' Sam said. 'He told us he was there to meet Rebecca Monteith. According to him she had hired him to find out about Marietta.' He registered a few raised eyebrows around the incident room. 'According to Paton, she believed Marietta was her daughter.'

'And is she?' DC Alan Rowe's brow creased. Sam could see the officer was going over the possibilities this might throw up.

'He was a bit vague on that,' Sam said, eyeing the clock above the whiteboard. 'I'm about to interview him again.'

He caught Will's eye. 'Can you speak to some of the students at Marietta's college and then meet me at her digs? We need to speak to that Elise again.'

'No problem,' Will said.

Sam thanked his team and they dispersed to their various

tasks while he went back to the interview room with DS Jake McAuley and DC Mark Owen.

Victor Paton was already there and looking more impatient by the second. He pulled an irritated expression as the three officers entered the room. 'How much longer are you going to keep me here?' he demanded. 'You know I have nothing to do with Rebecca's murder, or the disappearance of the Olsen girl. And while you're wasting your time with me the real killer is out there laughing at you.'

'We only have your word you were employed by the victim to collect information about Miss Olsen. No paperwork or contracts were found at the Falmouth Detective Agency.' Sam tilted his head to one side and looked at Paton. 'Why was that, Victor?'

The man's gaze slid away. 'I knew you'd come after me when I found Rebecca's body. The last person to see a murder victim is always the main suspect.' He paused and swallowed. 'I went back to the agency and grabbed everything that could have connected me to her and put it in a lock-up.'

'A lock-up?' Sam repeated.

'There's a filling station at the roundabout on the coast road leaving Falmouth. They have some lock-up units there.'

'And the key?'

'It's on the keyring your custody sergeant took from me with my other possessions when you arrested me.'

Sam nodded to Mark Owen and watched him leave the room to check out what the man had said before turning back to Paton. 'What I don't understand is why Rebecca would need you. Adopted children have the right to know their birth mother and I imagine Marietta may well have contacted her real mother eventually.'

A slow smile spread across Victor Paton's face. 'You don't know, do you?'

'Tell me.'

'Marietta was not adopted. She was sold.' He paused, enjoying the surprise on Sam's face. 'Back then Rebecca was a starving artist who had split from her husband.' He looked up with a sneering smile. 'Did you know by the way that he was a waiter at Trevere Manor?'

Sam's bland expression gave away nothing.

'You were telling me Rebecca sold her child,' he said curtly.

'That's right. She'd found this dodgy agency that fixed it all up. She wasn't supposed to know where the kid went, but the couple who'd been lined up to buy the kid had previously come to the home where the babies were born. Rebecca just happened to be listening at the door when the money was handed over. She heard them addressed as Mr and Mrs Olsen and Sweden mentioned.'

Sam shook his head. 'I'll ask again. If Rebecca knew all along who had bought her child then why did she need to employ you?'

'She didn't know, not for sure. Olsen isn't an unusual name in Sweden. And she was not aware of any connection with Bristol. It was me who discovered the Olsens ran a business in Bristol. Rebecca wanted absolute proof that Marietta was her daughter, which is why she wanted me to follow her. She was desperate for any scrap of information I could find.'

'Why didn't Rebecca come to us? It's illegal to buy and sell children in this country – and was even back then,' Sam said.

Victor Paton shrugged. 'She didn't want to distress Marietta. I think her plan was to make friends with the girl and get to know her that way.'

Sam's expression was stern. There had been no indication of a connection between Rebecca and Marietta until now. He narrowed his eyes. 'I don't understand. How did she know about Marietta? She wouldn't even have had her name.'

Victor's expression was blank. 'Don't ask me. It's not something she shared.'

It was another question for Will to ask the students. He needed to ring him.

'Well, what about me, Inspector? I've told you everything I know about your victim and your missing girl. Can I go now?'

Sam could think of no reason to continue detaining the man. 'You can go,' he said. 'But don't leave the area. We may need to speak to you again.'

Victor Paton released a loud sigh. 'At last. And as far as your accommodation goes, Inspector. I've known better.'

DC Owen had come back into the room with confirmation of Paton's lock-up key and Sam instructed him to take the man to be released.

Will had already left the incident room when Sam got back there. He rang his mobile and passed on the news of a connection between their missing girl and Rebecca Monteith. It was another thing to ask Marietta's landlady, Elise Clark, about.

CHAPTER 16

Isabella Mordaunt moved towards Sam and Will with the lightness of a young fawn. Sam thought she looked too young to be Marietta's tutor. She extended her hand to them. 'We are all absolutely broken-hearted about poor dear Rebecca. None of us can quite believe it's true. Who would do such a terrible thing?'

Sam couldn't hide his surprise. 'You knew Rebecca Monteith?'

'Of course I did. She was one of our visiting tutors. Our students loved her.'

Sam waited a beat to let this news sink in. He hadn't considered Rebecca might have had a connection to the college. They'd been focusing on her work at the Penzance Museum.

'So she had direct contact with the students?'

'Yes, of course she did.'

'Would one of those students have been Marietta Olsen?'

Isabella tucked a strand of dark hair behind her ear and smiled. 'Rebecca took a special interest in Marietta. She could see her potential. They used to meet and chat in our cafe. I think Marietta was inspired by Rebecca's encouragement of her work.'

'Were you aware that Marietta has disappeared?' Sam asked.

'What?' Isabella stared at him, the shock clear in her large dark eyes. 'What do you mean, disappeared? She was here at college yesterday…' She hesitated. 'Or was it Monday? No, it was Monday.' She blinked, frowning. 'Have her parents been informed?'

'That's been attended to,' Sam said. 'Can we see some of Marietta's work?' He was keen to get a deeper insight into what the girl was like. One thing he was learning was she was nothing like the young woman who trailed meekly in Cadan Tremayne's wake. Perhaps it was true she'd had enough of his arrogance and had simply bailed out. Her family was apparently wealthy, so she probably had the financial wherewithal to up and leave if that's what she wanted.

He stared at the display of Marietta's paintings, not quite understanding the wispy impressionist images of Cornish harbours.

'So much talent,' Isabella Mordaunt said, coming to stand next to him.

'Would you say she was the kind of student to turn her back on all of this and disappear?' His eyes were still on the missing girl's work.

'In my opinion, definitely not,' Isabella said. 'Why would she? She loves what she does. She's on her way to achieving a BA Hons in fine art and I know that means a lot to Marietta.'

Will had also been looking around. 'What kind of career could she have if she gained this degree?' he asked.

Isabella smiled. 'All our graduates leave Falmouth qualified to work across a wide sector of creativity. That could include employment with creative businesses, museum services and design studios. Some of our graduates have set up successful digital and online practices.'

'So, plenty of scope for a talented and qualified artist then?' he said.

Isabella nodded. 'Most definitely.'

Sam was imagining how different things must have been for Rebecca all those years ago. Despite her artistic talent she was so impoverished she'd been driven to sell her newborn child. Had that child really been Marietta? Could Marietta have discovered this? Was this why she had disappeared?

'You should speak to Marietta's friend,' Isabella said.

Sam frowned. 'I thought you told another officer Marietta was a loner and had no special friends here at college?'

Isabella looked embarrassed. 'I forgot about Elise. She works part time in our cafe.'

Sam and Will exchanged a look.

'Do you mean Elise Clark?' Sam said.

Isabella nodded. 'Yes, I think that's her name. She's older than Marietta but I did often see them talking and laughing together.'

'I THOUGHT they had an *all singing, all dancing*, security system in here,' Will said as he and Sam walked into the Penzance Museum later that day. The first attempt by persons unknown to break into the place might have failed, but whoever had carried out this second attempt had been more successful.

Jessica Liddle came hurrying to meet them. 'I can't believe this has happened,' she said. 'I'll take you to the gallery where the sketches were displayed.'

They followed her into a small room. Sam recognized drawings by Dame Laura Knight on the walls. Their eyes rested on the places where the stolen sketches had been. 'How did it happen, Miss Liddle?' Sam asked. 'Aren't all these works of art alarmed?'

Jessica Liddle gave an embarrassed nod. 'The thieves were crafty. They waited until we were closing. The smoke detectors went off and while we were busy evacuating the building the sketches were lifted from the wall. The place was in such disarray that these people were able to steal the pieces and walk out with them.' She gave a little cough. 'It wasn't easy to tell the owner what had happened.'

'The owner?' Sam enquired. But he already knew Loveday's friend, Priddy Rodda had loaned the sketches to the museum. The drawings were of her former neighbour, Jago Tilley's mother as a girl, sketched by the celebrated Cornish artist, Walter Langley. They had also got the old fisherman murdered. When he bequeathed the artwork to Priddy she passed it on to the museum explaining she wanted everyone to enjoy it.

'She was very upset, naturally,' Jessica Liddle continued. 'But confident the police would recover it.'

The first person who sprung into Sam's mind when Loveday told him about the theft had been Cadan. He had a history of stealing works of art, but he was already in a big enough tizzy about his missing girlfriend. Would he have been capable of carrying out the theft? On the other hand, his apparent distress over Marietta's disappearance could have been a planned distraction.

The more he thought about it, Cadan's anguish could have been a cover to disguise that it was him who had abducted the girl. They needed to speak to him again.

IN THE RECEPTION area of *Cornish Folk* magazine Cadan Tremayne was pacing the floor when Loveday arrived back from her lunch with Cassie. She stared at him in growing alarm. 'What's happened?'

'Nothing, that's the trouble. Nothing is going to happen unless we make it. I need your help, Loveday. We have to speak to the private eye.'

'Victor Paton? But why? The police have already spoken to him and from what I could gather they're satisfied he knows nothing about Marietta's disappearance.'

'And we are just supposed to believe that?' He gave her an

incredulous look. 'I've met the guy. I know what he's like. He'll speak to me, but I'll need a witness with me. I need you, Loveday.'

Loveday couldn't believe she was standing with Cadan at the door of the Falmouth Detective Agency. He didn't bother knocking before he burst in.

Victor Paton was sitting at a desk with the spectacular backdrop of the Carrick Roads visible from the window behind him. His initial surprise turned to suspicion as he narrowed his eyes at Cadan.

'I don't remember inviting you in,' he said, including Loveday in his disapproving stare.

'We need the truth, Paton. We're not the police, we just need to know where Marietta is.'

'You've come to the wrong bloke, mate. Ask the one who's taken her.'

'So you know she was taken?' Cadan said, advancing on the seated man.

Paton put up his hands in a gesture of defence. 'I told the cops and I'm telling you. I know nothing about this girl.'

'Stop lying.' Cadan's voice was rising. 'You were lucky I didn't give you a good hiding when I caught you skulking outside Marietta's flat that night. You were stalking her.

Don't tell me you're not involved in this.'

Loveday stepped forward before Cadan had a chance to grab the man by the throat. 'Please, Mr Paton. We really do need your help.' Loveday was throwing everything at appealing to the man's good nature. 'Marietta could be in danger. If there's anything… even the tiniest scrap of information, you must tell us.'

Victor Paton gave a deep sigh. 'Look. I was only doing my job. Rebecca Monteith wanted me to keep an eye on your girl. She had this idea Marietta was her daughter. It was my job to find something to back this up.'

Loveday blinked. 'Shouldn't it have been Marietta's parents you investigated?'

'That wasn't my brief. My client wanted to know where the girl went and who she met.' He slid a glance to Cadan. 'That was you mainly.'

'Who else did she meet, Victor?' Loveday asked, getting closer to him. 'Who else?'

'Nobody specific. She met loads of people at the college and the arty farty pub she went to here in Falmouth.' He paused and gave Loveday an unpleasant grin. 'And then there was this flatmate of hers. Now there's an accommodating female if ever I met one.'

'What does that mean?' Cadan said.

Paton gave a slow shrug. 'She saw me hanging around outside the house and asked what I was doing. We got talking. She invited me in for a drink.' He winked at Loveday. 'And things went my way if you know what I mean.'

Cadan frowned. 'Wait a minute. Are you saying you told Elise Clark you were investigating Marietta and she just invited you in?'

'Don't be thick. Of course I didn't. I told her it was one of her neighbours I was keeping an eye on. She liked that. She was taken with the idea of having a private eye in her bed.'

Loveday turned away to hide her revulsion of the man. She took a breath. 'I suppose you took full advantage of the opportunity to ask about Marietta. What did she tell you?'

Paton gave another shrug. 'Nothing I didn't already know.'

Cadan frowned. 'So that's it? That's all you can tell us?'

Paton pressed his lips together. 'There is something else, but I don't see how it will help you.'

'Try us,' Cadan said.

'There was a biker hanging around.'

'Biker?' Loveday saw Cadan's shoulders stiffen. He leaned menacingly close to Paton. 'What d'you mean, biker? What biker?'

'How the hell would I know,' Paton said. 'I wasn't being paid to watch him, just *her*.'

Loveday put out a hand. 'Let's get this straight. Are you saying Marietta was being followed by somebody on a motorbike?'

'That's exactly what it looked like.'

'Did you tell the police this?' Loveday said.

'Nope.'

'Why not?' Loveday was struggling to hold on to her patience.

Paton gave her his smirking smile again. 'They didn't ask.'

Cadan was glaring at the man like he was about to punch him, but Loveday stepped quickly forward and grabbed his arm. 'He's not worth it, Cadan. Come on. Let's get out of here.'

CHAPTER 17

Marietta froze! All her senses focused on that distant drone of an engine. Was it them? We're they coming back? She flew to the window, scratching with broken nails at the sliver of daylight between the rough wooden planks nailed there to block out the world. She put her eye to the slit but could only get an impression of bare twigs on nearby shrubs.

If the motorbike was coming back she wouldn't see it. But she could hear it – and it *was* coming back. She could hear it getting closer!

A wave of fear shuddered through her. Is this when she would die? Was the biker coming to kill her? She cowered in a corner, wrapping her thin arms around herself...and waited with pounding heart.

It was only minutes before she heard a door slam. There was the sound of footsteps on a stone floor and then a key turned in the lock and the door of her prison slowly scraped open. The figure in black biking leathers came into the room. 'Eat!' the gruff voice said, dropping a bulging supermarket bag on the floor. Marietta stared at the bag. She tried to think. If they were feeding her, maybe they weren't going to kill her. That made sense, didn't it? But they weren't letting her go!

Her effort to stay calm wasn't working. She could feel the fear inside her escalating into fury. Her captor was still standing there. She rushed at them, striking out with flying fists. 'Let me out of here,' she screamed. 'Why are you doing this?'

Startled eyes stared at her through the dark visor of a helmet as the biker's arms came up, fending off the attack.

The figure began to back out of the room, but Marietta came again, making a grab for the helmet. 'Why are you hiding yourself?' she yelled, her face contorted with rage. 'Who are you?'

The push she got in return sent Marietta flying back and she crashed painfully against the wall, sending her sliding to the floor. For a second the biker stood glaring down at her and then backed silently out of the room.

Marietta lifted her head, her shoulders slumping in defeat as the key turned in the lock. She'd been shut in again. A tear slid down her face. Where was Cadan? Where was Elise? Where were all the people who were supposed to care about her? She began to sob. She was being left to die in this filthy, dark hole and she didn't know why.

IN THE LANE OUTSIDE, the biker roared away, speeding through village trying to erase that look of despair in the girl's eyes as she pleaded for her release. But it wasn't up to the biker. The whole thing was spiralling out of control, but this wasn't the time to give in to nerves. They had to go through with it now. They'd come too far.

A few people looked up as the motorbike swung past the caravans and came to a halt outside a slightly shabby one. Inside the biker removed the helmet and flung it on the bed, pushing fingers through the stubbly, cropped hair. The whole thing was going badly. This isn't what they'd signed up for. The biker tore off the leathers and paced the confined space impatiently before turning and striding out of the caravan, heading for the coastal path.

The waves were crashing over the white sand and the figure walked on, looking out towards the blackening sky. The phone in the biker's pocket buzzed and they fished it out of a trouser pocket, frowned as the name of the caller came up.

'Just checking everything's OK,' the voice said.

'Well it isn't! I'm not sure I can do this any longer.' The biker's voice trembled. 'You *do* know we won't get away with this?'

'Get a grip of yourself,' the caller snapped back. 'You're in this as deep as me. Nobody's backing out. Do you understand? Besides,' the voice was silky soft now. 'Think of all that lovely lolly when the Olsens cough up.'

'You don't seriously think we'll see any of that? The cops will be in charge of everything. The Olsens won't get the chance to do what you say, even if they wanted to.'

'Oh, they'll want to all right,' the caller said. 'We have their little girl…remember?'

'How can I forget? I'm the one who has to face her. She's fighting back now. She came at me today and almost knocked me out.'

The voice gave a rasping laugh. 'Don't tell me you're frightened of a little girl? I thought you were the tough guy.'

'I'm not going soft if that's what you think, but this girl's not stupid. She hears me coming and she gets ready to fly at me as soon as the door opens.' The biker gave an impatient sigh. 'What I'm saying is every time I go into that stinking room it gives her another shot at trying to escape.'

'Take double rations next time,' the voice came back. 'And then you'll only need to check up on her every *second* day.'

'That's what I did,' came the sharp retort. 'I'll ask again. How much longer are we going to keep this up?'

'Not much longer,' the caller assured. 'Not now the Olsens are here in Cornwall. I know where they're staying. A note will be pushed under the door of their room before they get up in the morning. It will remind them again what will happen to their precious Marietta if they don't do what they're told.'

'They'll never pay half a million. It's a crazy idea. You're crazy. I should never have got mixed up in this.'

'Well, you did, and you're stuck with it. So don't go getting any stupid ideas or you'll see a very different side of me.'

'Are you threatening me?'

'Not yet, but I'll be doing more than threatening if this goes belly up because you're too much of a milksop to see it through. And don't think you could hide because I'd come after you. What I will do to you won't be pleasant.'

The biker shivered, knowing the chilling words were no empty threat.

The caller hadn't finished. 'But it won't come to that, will it?' A pause. 'Stop thinking of things that could go wrong. It won't happen. The Olsens are rich. They can afford half a million. They'll stump up all right.'

The biker could tell the caller was smiling now. The excitement of laying their hands on all that money had taken over again. This was getting more frightening by the minute. 'OK, tell me exactly how we pick up the ransom under the cops' noses? Even if the Olsens co-operate and agree to taking the cash to a drop-off point, the old bill will be all over it like a rash.'

'It won't happen, but if it does then we will deal with it,' the caller said. 'Don't worry. I've planned everything. We'll hit them when they least expect it.'

'And what about the girl? Will you really let her go?'

'Of course I will.'

But the words came too quickly.

There had been a struggle when they'd grabbed Marietta in that car park and the balaclava the biker's accomplice had been wearing had almost been torn off. Marietta could have seen the other one's face before the chloroform-soaked rag was clamped over her nose. It had been audacious to capture the girl and drive her off in her own car, but it's what they did.

The yellow car was hidden in one of the outhouses beside the cottage where they were holding her. And they had driven off on the motorbike. Apart from the business with the balaclava, it had been an efficient exercise. But the mask incident couldn't be ignored. Marietta may have seen enough to be able to identify her kidnapper. She hadn't said so, but they couldn't be sure. The biker knew what must be in the other kidnapper's mind. If Marietta could identify them there could be no option. Whether they got the ransom money or not, the Olsen girl would have to die!

CHAPTER 18

'Motorbike?' Sam stared at her. Loveday could see he was furious with her for going with Cadan to find Victor Paton. 'I think you'd better explain yourself,' he said.

Loveday took a deep breath. She knew she had to justify her decision. 'Cadan came to see me. He was desperate and you had already interviewed Paton. We thought he was no longer a suspect.'

'While a case is ongoing everyone is a suspect. You know that.' Sam glared at her.

Loveday pulled an apologetic face. 'Maybe we shouldn't have gone to see Paton, but he told us about the biker.'

'What exactly did he tell you?'

'OK, it wasn't much, only that he'd noticed a motorbike in the vicinity of Marietta's digs. I guess he thought it was around too often to be a co-incidence.'

'Maybe it was a neighbour who had a motorbike,' Sam said.

'Perhaps, but I got the impression Victor Paton didn't think so.'

'Is there anything else I should know?'

'Actually, there is. Although I'm not sure how important this might be.'

'I'm listening,' Sam said.

'Marietta's flatmate, Elise somebody, slept with Paton.'

Sam frowned and Loveday could tell that piece of information had surprised him. 'Oh, did she now?' he said slowly. 'So they're in a relationship?'

'I think it was more of a one-night stand. Paton was boasting about it. Apparently this Elise had noticed him hanging around outside and went to challenge him. He lied through his teeth of course and told her he was keeping surveillance on one of her neighbours.' She paused. 'According to Paton, Elise accepted his story, but more than that, she was quite taken with the fact he was a private eye. She invited him into the flat for a drink – and he stayed the night. At least that's his story, but he volunteered it, so I don't see why he would lie.'

'Was Marietta there?'

'He says not. Cadan had picked her up earlier. He'd been about to call it a night when Elise came out.'

She tilted her head at him. 'I didn't mean to step on anyone's toes, Sam. Would you believe me if I said I was sorry.'

'What do you think?' His tone was still angry.

'Aren't you a little bit pleased? We found out about that motorbike. You should talk to Victor Paton again.'

'Thank you for the advice,' Sam said. 'Now could you please stay out of the case and leave the police work to me?'

Loveday took a deep breath. 'I'm sorry, Sam,' she said quietly, watching his face for any sign he had calmed down. She waited a beat before going on. 'What about the motorbike thing? Could it be important?'

He blew out his cheeks. 'Possibly,' he said, reaching for his phone. 'Malcolm Carter and Alan Rowe are the late duty men tonight. I'll get them to check out motorbike owners in Cornwall.' He sighed. 'There'll be thousands of them.'

'There will be biker clubs too,' Loveday offered and then held up her hands in defence as Sam lowered his eyebrows at her.

She cleared away their supper dishes, trying not to listen to Sam's instructions to his detectives as he moved into the other room. She'd known he would not be happy about her going with Cadan to speak to the private eye, but she hadn't expected him to be quite so angry with her. She consoled herself with the hope that he might track down the biker Paton had mentioned. It was still no guarantee that it would help them find Marietta, but it was surely something.

Loveday was sitting at the table nursing a mug of coffee when Sam came back into the kitchen. He went to the fridge and took out a bottle of Doom Bar.

'Any more news on Priddy's sketches?' she asked as he poured his drink into a pint glass. 'And before you tell me to mind my own business, my friends are my business. Priddy was very upset when she rang to tell me they had been stolen.'

'Yes, I'm sorry about that. I know how important those drawings of Jago's mother are to both her and the museum.'

Loveday sipped her coffee. 'How can a couple of pictures be stolen in broad daylight? Surely a museum that has all those important paintings must have an effective security system?'

'They do.' Sam sighed. 'Whoever took the sketches chose his time well. The place was about to close and staff were ushering visitors out when the fire alarm went off. Whether it was part of the thief's plan or a badly timed coincidence, we don't know. Anyway the building had to be evacuated and when staff returned they discovered the Walter Langley sketches had been snatched.'

The thought that was going through Loveday's head was so obvious as to be ridiculous. There was one person who might feel entitled to steal those drawings.

'I suppose you've considered Jago's nephew, Billy Travis? He led old Jago a merry dance when he was alive.'

'We're on to it,' Sam said.

The last Loveday had heard of the man he'd been living rough in an old caravan at the back of Marazion. He'd known about the drawings of Jago's mother and how valuable they were. According to Priddy, he still felt aggrieved that Jago had bequeathed the sketches to her. As Jago's only living relative he believed they should have come to him.

'We had detectives in Marazion today trying to find him. He wasn't in his caravan, but I have a feeling he's still around here. I'll do a bit of sniffing about in the morning.'

'I could go with you to talk to Priddy,' Loveday offered. 'And before you say no, it would make sense. Priddy knows me better than she knows you. She'll be more relaxed if I'm there.'

Sam grimaced, but she could see he knew the idea was practical.

'I can't stop thinking about Marietta's poor parents. They must be frantic for news,' Loveday said later as she got into bed.

'Nils and Giselle Olsen arrived in Cornwall this afternoon. Amanda has been keeping an eye on them. She'll introduce herself when the time is right.'

'Amanda?' Loveday gave him a surprised look.

'I know what you're thinking, but sometimes Amanda surprises people.'

'She's not the most compassionate member of your team,' Loveday said, remembering the times she had witnessed the woman's gruff attitude to witnesses.

'I've had a quiet word with her. She will be sensitive to the Olsens' situation. I'll be speaking to them myself tomorrow.'

'Have they admitted lying when they said Marietta had gone to a retreat in Sweden?'

'Not according to Amanda,' Sam said, leaning in for a kiss as he slipped under the duvet. 'But they've come to Cornwall for a reason and I believe that reason is to find their daughter.'

A thought struck Loveday. 'I wonder if Cadan should speak to

Marietta's parents?' But Sam's look of disapproval answered that. 'OK, bad idea,' she conceded.

The sun was shining as they left the cottage next morning. Out in Mounts Bay a light breeze was rippling the surface of the water. 'I understand Priddy is very upset about her sketches,' Sam said.

Loveday pouted as he turned the Lexus into the lane that led to Storm Cottage. 'I would say she's more angry than upset. She fully expects you to recover them.'

'I'm flattered by her confidence in me.'

Loveday slid him a look as they got out of the car and went to knock on the cottage door. 'I wouldn't get too smug if I were you. Priddy can be a fearsome adversary if people let her down.'

The door opened almost immediately and the delicious smell of newly made scones wafted out at them. 'I hope this means you've got some good news for me about those sketches,' Priddy said, her blue eyes shifting from one to the other.

'See what I mean?' Loveday giggled.

'I'm sorry, not yet,' Sam said, trying not to sound sheepish as they followed her into the warm kitchen. 'We were hoping you might be able to help.'

Priddy screwed up her face. 'How can I do that? I don't know who stole Jago's mother.'

Loveday had to hide a smile at her friend's description of the acclaimed Walter Langley sketches. 'We were wondering if Billy Travis has been around recently?' she said. Out of the corner of her eye she saw Sam frown and realized she should have left the questions to him.

'Billy? No,' Priddy said. 'He never comes down here now Jago's gone. No reason to you see. There's no one to scrounge off any more.' Her blue eyes widened and she turned to stare at Sam. 'Wait a minute. Are you saying he had something to do with this?'

'We don't know,' Sam said. 'We have some questions for him, that's all.'

Priddy bit her lip, thinking. 'I doubt if he even knew the sketches were in the museum. He probably thinks I sold them.'

'Do you know where he works?' Sam asked.

'He's employed by that construction firm. He drives a digger up on the building site behind the school.'

Sam checked his watch. 'They should have started work by now.'

Priddy's face dropped. 'You're not going?' She indicated the rack of fruit scones cooling on the table. 'I can't eat all these by myself.'

Sam smiled. 'Maybe Loveday could help you there.'

Priddy turned her attention hopefully to Loveday. 'You don't have to go as well, do you?'

'Sorry, Priddy, I have to get to work, but I don't mind taking some of those off your hands. I can think of one or two people at the office who would be delighted to sample your baking.'

Priddy went to a drawer and took out a plastic bag, which she filled with scones. 'Take them with pleasure, Loveday.' She turned to Sam. 'Please tell me you'll get Jago's mother back.'

'We'll do our best, Priddy.' Sam flashed his most reassuring smile.

'Ah, well.' The old lady sighed, following them to the door. 'Just see that you do.'

Sam dropped Loveday off at the cottage to collect her car. On his way to the building site he got a call from Will. 'Looks like our stolen sketches have turned up. We've had a call from an antiques shop in Penzance. A man brought them in yesterday and the owner's assistant paid him £250. He says the young woman recognized the Langley's signature, but she didn't realize the significance of the sketches. She hadn't even been aware they were stolen.'

'I'm only minutes away from there now,' Sam said. 'What's the shop owner's name?'

'It's a Ronnie Burcott,' Will came back.

'Give me the address. I'll go and see him.'

The antiques shop was a small, overcrowded green-painted premises in Church Street. Sam parked at the door and went in.

The tinkle of the bell brought a short, grey-haired man from a back room. He smiled at Sam. 'Feel free to browse,' he said. 'If there's anything I can help with, please ask.'

'Ronnie Burcott?' Sam produced his warrant card and the man raised an eyebrow. 'Ah, you'll be here about the sketches.'

'I'd like to see them,' Sam said.

The man disappeared into the back room and returned with the framed drawings. 'Are these what you've been looking for?' He handed them over.

The last time Sam had seen the sketches they were in a plastic supermarket bag that Loveday and Priddy had retrieved from the shed where Jago had hidden them from his grasping nephew, Billy Travis.

Sam ran his eyes over them. He was no expert, but they looked like the real thing.

'Is your assistant here?' he asked. 'I'd like a word.'

'Greta! can you come through here?' Ronnie Burcott called.

A young woman with long, straight brown hair and a wary look in her dark eyes appeared.

Sam smiled. 'You are Miss...?'

'I'm Greta Blewitt,' the girl said cautiously.

'And you purchased these sketches yesterday?'

She slid a panicked look to her employer.

'Just tell him, Greta,' Burcott said.

'I recognized the signature. I'd been reading up on the Newlyn School of Artists, Walter Langley, Stanhope Forbes and the others. I thought what I was seeing was previously undiscovered sketches.

The man said they belonged to his uncle and had been in their family for years.'

'Can you describe this man?' Sam asked, although he was in no doubt who this was.

'Thin, bald, late thirties. Very scruffy looking,' Greta said. 'He wanted £500 for them. I gave him £250.' She threw an apologetic look to her employer. 'Did I do something awful? Mr Burcott said the sketches were stolen from a gallery.'

Sam sighed. 'We'll have to check out the authenticity but yes, it could be the ones we've been looking for.'

'Am I in trouble? Will I be charged with buying stolen goods?'

Ronnie Burcott put an arm around his assistant. 'I'm sure it won't come to that. You're helping the police. We both are.' He looked at Sam for confirmation.

'We might require you to come into the station to make a formal statement, and identify the man who sold these, but if what you've told me is true and you continue to co-operate with us, you won't be charged with anything.'

Greta Blewitt's face cracked into a relieved smile. 'Thank you,' she said.

Sam tucked the sketches under his arm as he left the shop, his free hand reaching for his phone. 'Bring Billy Travis in,' he said when Will answered. 'He has some explaining to do.'

CHAPTER 19

'Cadan Tremayne is downstairs, sir,' DC Amanda Fox said as she poked her head around the door of Sam's office.

'Put him in an interview room. I'll be down directly.' After a day of searching for Marietta they were no further forward. He wasn't looking forward to appraising Cadan of the situation. Merrick's half-brother would be looking for answers and he had none to give.

Sam took a deep breath before entering the interview room. Cadan was pacing the floor but stopped as Sam came in and wheeled round to face him.

'Before you say anything, Cadan. We have every man and woman we can spare out looking for Marietta. Her parents have arrived in Cornwall and I'll be speaking to them later.'

'You know they lied about Marietta being in Sweden,' Cadan said. There was excitement in his voice. 'I already knew the Olsens were here in Truro.'

Sam stared at him. 'And how do you know this?'

'I've seen them. And I can tell you where they're staying.'

Sam raised an eyebrow. He already knew this from Amanda but he was interested to hear what Cadan had to say.

'They've booked into Bartons Hotel. I've seen them going in.'

Sam gestured towards the chair. 'OK, let's take this slowly. Tell me what you saw.'

The man sat down but he was still fidgeting excitedly. 'I was on my way to see Loveday when I saw them coming out of the bank in Boscawen Street. It's a while since I've been in their company, but it was definitely them. They didn't see me, so I followed them. I was excited and filled with dread at the same time.' He looked up. 'What are they doing here, Sam?'

'I don't know. We'll find out. Go on.'

'I followed them to the corner and they turned up to Bartons Hotel. I watched them go into reception and saw them collect their room key. But they're not using their own name. I checked. They've booked in under the names of Celine and Erik Larsson.' He met Sam's eyes. 'Now why would they do that?'

'That's going to be my first question,' Sam said.

'Can I come with you? I know them.'

'No, you have to leave this to us,' Sam said. 'Go home now, Cadan. We'll keep you informed, I promise.'

Sam could have issued instructions for the Olsens to be picked up from the hotel, but he wanted to be there himself. He wanted to see their reaction when the police turned up.

He decided not to visit the Olsens mob handed. If their daughter had been kidnapped, which was looking increasingly likely, the couple would need sensitive handling. There was also the possibility Marietta's abductors were watching the hotel.

Sam parked in the busy street and he and Will got out. The Bartons was a friendly boutique hotel set in a Georgian townhouse. Sam had never stayed there but the proximity of its adjoining wine bar to the offices of the *Cornish Folk* magazine made it a popular eating place for Loveday and her colleagues.

Sam and Will showed their ID to the receptionist. 'Can you

ring your guests, Mr and Mrs Larsson, and ask them to come down to reception. No need to mention the police.'

The receptionist's unsure look went from one to the other as she lifted the phone and spoke to the Olsens. Sam told Will to take a seat as he kept an eye on the narrow stairs, waiting for the couple to come down. They appeared within minutes and had such looks of apprehension that Sam's heart went out to them.

He stepped forward, showing his warrant card to them. 'Mr and Mrs Olsen? Can you come with us, please?'

Giselle Olsen's fine bony hand went to her throat and the other grabbed her husband's arm.

'I think you're mistaken,' Nils Olsen said. 'Our name is Larsson. The receptionist will tell you.'

'We know who you are,' Sam said gently. 'We want to help you, but you have to trust us.'

Will joined the group. 'We need to speak to you,' he said quietly.

'This is not helpful. You don't know what's going on,' Nils Olsen said.

'Believe me, sir. We do.'

Giselle Olsen was now openly tearful.

Sam glanced around him, uncomfortable about this being discussed in such a public place. 'We're here to protect your daughter, Mrs Olsen,' Sam said quietly. 'We have a car outside. Can you please come with us?'

Amanda had done her best to settle the Olsens in the interview room but by the look of anguish on the couple's faces she hadn't succeeded. Nils was already pacing the room and Giselle leapt to her feet as Sam and Will entered.

Sam's smile was compassionate. 'We understand what a difficult time this must be for both of you, but please be assured we are doing everything we can to find Marietta.'

'Are you?' Giselle Olsen gave Sam a hostile stare. 'I thought Cornwall was a safe place. How could our daughter simply disappear? Is this how you look after your people here?' Nils put a hand on his wife's arm. 'My wife is distraught…we both are. We just want our daughter back.'

Sam gave an understanding nod. 'We all want that, Mr Olsen, but we need your help. We need to know all about Marietta.'

'What do you want to know?'

'Let's start at the beginning. Were you living in Bristol when your daughter was born?' Sam had no intention of confronting them with the allegation they had illegally acquired Rebecca Monteith's child – not yet – but he was interested in how they would deal with his questions.

'Marietta is adopted,' Giselle said curtly, her eyes nervously straying to the wall clock.

'Do you know who her birth mother is?'

'No. We never wanted to know that. She is *our* daughter.'

'So Marietta doesn't know she's adopted,' Will said.

'We saw no reason to tell her,' Nils said. 'She was so happy here in Cornwall. She loves her life as a student at the art college.'

'She gave no hint anything was wrong?' Sam asked.

Giselle's head snapped up. 'Nothing was wrong. Marietta hasn't run away. Something has happened to her. You should be out looking.'

Sam's brow wrinkled into a frown. 'What do you think has happened to her, Mrs Olsen?'

Giselle threw up her hands in frustration. 'How would I know? That's your job, Inspector. All I know is our daughter is out there somewhere, possibly injured, probably very frightened. You have to find her.'

Sam was watching the couple. The woman was checking her watch again.

'If you have any more questions for us you need to ask them quickly,' Nils Olsen said. 'My wife is not strong. She needs to rest. I want to get her back to the hotel as quickly as possible.' He was getting to his feet. 'If you have any other questions is where you will find us.'

He put a hand on his wife's elbow and helped her to her feet. 'I take it you have no objection if we leave now?'

All three detectives exchanged a look.

'Please sit down, Mr Olsen,' Sam said. 'We can't help you unless you trust us. Let me tell you what we believe is going on. Marietta's abductors have contacted you and demanded a ransom. You've been seen coming out of a Truro bank. Have you collected the ransom money?'

Nils Olsen bit his lip. His wife was shaking her head at him. 'Don't tell them, Nils. They'll kill her.' She had started to sob. 'They said they would kill her…'

The couple hugged each other, rocking back and forward. Sam stretched out a hand to touch them. 'We'll find Marietta, but you must tell us everything.'

Nils took a deep breath and rubbed his hands over his face. 'We were contacted two days ago. They spoke to my wife and said they had Marietta and would kill her if we contacted the police. They told us to make up a story if anyone came looking for Marietta. We were instructed to come to Cornwall and book into Bartons Hotel.'

Sam's brow creased as he took all this in. 'They told you to say your daughter had gone off to a retreat in Sweden?' he said.

Nils shook his head. 'No, was my idea. We didn't want any of Marietta's friends reporting her as missing. We thought that explanation would satisfy everyone.'

'How much of a ransom have they demanded?'

'£500,000,' Nils said.

Amanda gave an involuntary gasp.

Sam fired her a look. 'Could you raise that much?' he asked.

Nils shrugged. 'It meant putting the business up as collateral, but yes, we have raised the money – only just.'

Sam's eyebrow shot up. 'Are you saying you have the ransom money here in town?'

'That's right,' Nils said. 'It's in the safe in our hotel room. This is the day we are supposed to hand it over. We have to put it in a Sainsbury's carrier bag and leave it in a bin in a designated position inside the Eden Project at exactly 4 o'clock.'

Everyone's eyes went to the wall clock. It was almost midday. They didn't have much time to act.

Giselle raised watery blue eyes to Sam. 'They said Marietta would be in the boot of a car in the car park. If the handover went as planned they would release her. If not…' She gave a whimper. 'They would drive off with her and we would never see our daughter again.'

Sam had never been forced to organize a stake-out at such short notice, but if they were going to find Marietta they had to pull out all the stops. A young woman's life was in jeopardy. They couldn't afford a mistake.

Amanda was told to escort the Olsens back to their hotel. Plain clothes officers would follow them later to the drop in an unmarked car.

Sam gathered the team together in the incident room and quickly outlined the situation.

Will pinned up a map of the Eden Project layout, focusing in particular on the network of footpaths from the various car parks to the main centre. He put a red cross on the bin the abductors had specified for the ransom drop.

'I know we've had virtually no time to plan this, but we are professionals.' His eyes travelled over the sea of faces gathered around him. 'This is the best team I have ever worked with. I know you can do this. Our priority is Marietta Olsen and returning her safely to her family.'

'What about the ransom, sir?' Malcolm Carter asked. 'Do we

concentrate on preventing the kidnappers getting their hands on it?'

An image of the Chief Constable's face if he had to explain how he'd lost the Olsens' £500,000 floated into Sam's mind. He quickly dismissed it. There would be time for recriminations later if things went wrong. But none of them could afford to let that happen.

'We obviously don't want them getting away with the ransom, but more importantly there's no question of allowing the kidnappers to escape. They're the only ones who know where Marietta is.'

He looked across the room to Will Tregellis. 'Can you fill the team in about the details of the drop?'

'Each of you will be given a copy of this map. Make a mental note of the lie of the land.' He jabbed a marker pen at the map and allocated each detective to a stake-out point.

'We need to be thinking on our feet with this one,' Sam cut in. 'We'll have another ten uniform officers in plain clothes backing us up. Keep cool heads, everybody. We can do this.'

They drove to the Eden Project in a convoy of cars. Will had already alerted the site owners to what was happening and had been assured of their full co-operation.

It was a few minutes past 2 o'clock when they arrived at St Austell. Sam had been timing the journey. It took just over half an hour, with a few minutes extra to negotiate their way through the site. It was crucial the Olsens didn't encounter any traffic problems.

The litter bin the kidnappers had chosen for the drop was identical to the others, but when he looked closer he saw that a white rag had been tied to the side of it. Had this been the kidnappers' way of making sure the Olsens found the right bin? Their planning had been ridiculously simple, childlike even. They had led the Olsens all the way, attended to every detail, right down to telling them which hotel to book into.

Sam frowned. Why did it have to be that hotel? And then it came to him in a flash. They were in the wrong place! The drop wasn't being made at this site. It was back in Truro – at Bartons Hotel!

He grabbed Will's arm and began striding to his car. 'I want everyone here to do exactly as you've been instructed,' he called over his shoulder. 'Keep your wits about you. The sergeant and I need to check out something.'

Will hurried after him, looking as confused as the team they'd left behind. 'What's going on, sir?' he said as they got into the Lexus and Sam threw the car into gear and sped out of the car park.

'I think we've got this all wrong, Will. This place was never intended as the ransom drop. It was a decoy. I think they're going to snatch the money from the Olsens somewhere between here and Truro.'

'Oh, God! What can we do?'

'I'm not sure. I might be wrong, which is why I left the team in situ back there. We have to think quick. If you were going to intercept a car and rob the occupants, where would you choose?'

'Well, not the main road,' Will said. 'Too many people about, too much chance of being caught.'

'So where?' Sam fired back. 'Think, Will…think!'

'Emm, I suppose the best place would be the hotel.'

'Exactly,' Sam said. 'They're going to grab the ransom when the Olsens leave the hotel.'

Sam had put his foot down and they were now speeding through the streets of Truro. 'Alert Amanda,' he shouted. 'And get hold of the escort car!' But they were already turning down into Lemon Street and hurtling towards the hotel.

The Lexus screeched to a halt as the Olsens were emerging from the building. Sam and Will jumped out and raced towards the couple. The motorbike came from nowhere, flashing past them as the rider make a grab for the bag of cash in Nils' hand. A woman screamed. A man launched himself at the rider, sending the motorbike in one direction and the rider flying in another. Sam and Will reacted immediately, but the biker was already scrambling up and taking off at speed towards the busy shopping centre. They gave chase. They couldn't let this person escape. But once they were amongst the shoppers it was impossible to spot the biker. 'Where the hell is he?' Sam shouted. The two detectives stood in the middle of Boscawen Street, frantically scanning the crowd. 'I don't know. I didn't see,' Will said.

Sam slapped his hand against a shop wall. The biker had disappeared…vanished into thin air.

Amanda was out of breath when she reached them. 'At least they didn't get the money,' she said. 'And neither of the Olsens is hurt.'

Sam's shoulders slumped as they turned slowly back to the hotel. A small crowd had gathered. One of the two officers in the escort car was leading the Olsens back into the hotel. The other was kneeling down beside the man who had hurled himself at the biker. The injured man raised his head and gave the officers a pleading look. 'Tell me you caught him.'

Sam looked down at the man who was bleeding on the ground and shook his head. 'Sorry, Cadan.'

CHAPTER 20

Loveday took pride in being last to leave the office. It had been an exhausting day. She had been busy blocking out columns for the article on page 10 and was straightening her desk before going when Cassie rang.

'Are you still in Truro?'

'Not for much longer,' Loveday said, pulling on her coat as she balanced the phone between her shoulder and ear. 'Why?'

'I wondered if you fancied taking the long way home and dropping into Falmouth to join me for a drink?'

Loveday's eye went to the clock. It was 5.30. Sam probably wouldn't be home before 9 o'clock.

Cassie caught the hesitation. 'Don't worry if you can't, it was only an idea. I've been cooped up on the *Three Graces* yacht on my own all afternoon sketching out its refurb plan.'

Loveday grinned. 'And you're now suffering from cabin fever?'

'Got it in one,' Cassie said with a sigh. 'That's exactly how I'm feeling. Are you sure you can't join me down here? Think of it as social work.'

'Put like that how can I refuse?' Loveday laughed.

'Brilliant,' Cassie said. 'Do you know the Captain's Table down by the harbour?'

'I do,' Loveday said as she headed down the back stairs to the staff car park. 'But I have another idea. I've been told about this place called the Brush and Pen. It's a pub down on The Moor.'

'Fine by me,' Cassie said. 'But I wouldn't have thought it was your kind of place.'

'Why?' Loveday asked.

'You'll see,' Cassie said. There was a smile in her voice.

Spaces in The Moor car park were at a premium during the day because it was so handy for the shops and town centre. But at this time of evening Loveday was spoiled for choice.

The Brush and Pen was long and dark and crammed with mis-matched furniture. It was also extremely busy, but Cassie had found a corner table and waved to catch her attention as she came in.

Like the other tables it was identified by a number attached to a well-stained paint brush in a glass. Loveday's eye was drawn to the corn dollies attached to the black beams and the scattering of pencil and charcoal sketches pinned around the walls. None of the oil paintings on display were framed. It was an odd place but curiously engaging.

'Are you thinking same as me? This place is weird,' Cassie said, getting up to go to the bar.

'Just coffee for me,' Loveday called after her as her friend made her way to the bar.

A black and white photograph of snowdrops and miniature daffodils growing around the base of an old tree was propped on a ledge above their table. The caption read *'Appreciate our wild flowers by leaving them where they grow'*.

Loveday sat back soaking up the atmosphere and enjoying the buzz of conversations all around her.

This was one of the places Cadan checked out when he was searching for Marietta. It was also the pub Victor Paton had mentioned where Marietta's flatmate, Elise Clark, worked. Loveday turned her attention to the bar staff. Could Elise be one of the barmaids she could see now? There was no way of knowing unless she actually went up and asked them and she wouldn't be doing that. She was already in enough trouble with Sam for her and Cadan's little escapade with the private eye.

She could see two women and a man behind the bar. All of them appeared to be working flat out serving an ever increasing number of customers. She tried to imagine which of the two women Marietta would have got on with, but then maybe she hadn't. Perhaps a dispute with Elise was what tipped the balance and Marietta really had gone off to the retreat somewhere.

'Come on, Elise! I was there before him. How long do you have to wait around here to get served?' Loveday stretched her neck to get a look at the impatient speaker, but she was more interested to see which barmaid responded to him. She didn't have to wait long. The woman who turned and wagged a warning finger at him had to be Elise. 'You'll wait your turn like the rest of them,' she said.

Loveday watched with interest as the woman pulled pints and poured wine into glasses before passing them across the bar. Her non-descript brown hair was scraped back into a stubby ponytail, which emphasized the sharp contours of her nose and chin. The overall effect gave her make-up free face a cross look.

Cassie was returning, balancing two white porcelain coffee mugs on a small tray. She sank down on the chair opposite. 'It's survival of the fittest over there. I've never seen a pub so busy at this time of day.'

She passed a mug to Loveday and eyed up the room. 'I suppose it's got something if you favour sandals and sticking flowers in your hair.' She sniffed the air. 'And something decidedly dodgy to smoke.'

'I know.' Loveday laughed. 'I got that too as soon as I came in.'

She leaned forward. 'It doesn't seem to be bothering anybody, not even the staff.'

Cassie grinned. 'Maybe it's lucky you didn't bring Sam with you. Why did you want to come here anyway?'

'No reason, well except I was curious to see the place. Apparently it's Marietta's local.'

'Yes I can see how she would fit in here. It's her kind of place.' Cassie took a sip of her coffee. 'Has Cadan managed to track her down yet?'

Loveday frowned. 'I'm not supposed to talk about it.'

'You've got me even more interested now,' Cassie said. 'Is it anything to do with that retreat you said she might have gone to?'

Loveday was making a mighty effort steer her friend away from that issue. She had no wish to suggest Marietta's parents had been lying. She nodded towards the bar. 'That woman with her hair tied back is Marietta's flatmate.'

Cassie gave her a surprised look. 'How on earth do you know that?'

'My amazing powers of deduction, well that and the fact I heard someone call her by name.'

Her friend's attention was on the bar now. It wasn't as busy as before and Elise appeared to be in earnest conversation with a customer. 'Is it my imagination,' Cassie said, 'or do you agree those two are on the verge of having the mother and father of all rows?'

Loveday chewed her bottom lip and frowned as she watched the women. The customer at the bar was gripping the beer glass in front of her so tightly Loveday was afraid it might shatter, flinging shards of glass everywhere. Elise was leaning in close to the woman, her expression angry. Whatever she was saying didn't seem to be pacifying the customer. At first Loveday thought it was a man, but when she caught sight of her face in profile she realized it was a woman.

The other two bar staff who had disappeared ten minutes

earlier when the peak busy time was over had returned. One of them nodded for Elise to take a break. She glanced quickly around the room and apparently satisfied that she and the customer were not the centre of attention indicated the disgruntled woman should follow her to the end of the bar. Loveday watched as Elise lifted the hatch and ushered the woman through. Intrigued by what might be going on she knew she had to find out more.

'I'll be back in a minute, Cassie,' she said. 'I need to have a quick word with someone.' She lifted her phone. 'I'll be right back.'

She knew Cassie was staring after her as she left the pub. The collection of beer barrels at the back of the building suggested this was close to the back door. She waited until it opened, and the two women emerged into the alley. Loveday edged back, squeezing her body into another doorway. Elise was touching the other woman's face, speaking softly to her, trying to coax her out of her previous mood. She held her breath as the two embraced – and then kissed.

Loveday drew back, embarrassed. She felt like a voyeur. This was clearly a tender moment between the two women. Judging by how they kissed they were far more to each other than merely friends. She took advantage of their total engrossment in each other to creep away unnoticed.

Loveday was surprised to see the cottage lit up and Sam's car in the drive when she and Cassie convoyed to Marazion later that evening. He was slumped in his chair staring into the fire. 'Something bad's happened, hasn't it? Is it Marietta?' She wasn't sure she wanted to hear the answer.

'You could say that,' Sam said, reaching for the whisky glass by his chair. He threw back the contents and gave Loveday a blow by blow description of the afternoon's events.

'Oh, Sam. I'm so sorry.' She put a hand on his shoulder. 'It wasn't your fault.'

'That's not how the Olsens see it. In their eyes I've killed their daughter.'

'What nonsense. We don't know what's happened to Marietta. Perhaps the abductors will try again?'

'I don't think so.'

'At least we now know she hasn't gone to a retreat. It could be argued the Olsens brought all this down on their own heads. Maybe if they had contacted you in the first place instead of lying and saying Marietta was at some hideaway things could be very different tonight,' Loveday argued. 'They totally compromised your efforts to find their daughter.'

She watched Sam get up and go to pour himself another whisky. He brought the glass back and put it down with a sigh. 'They're not to blame. The kidnappers warned them not contact the police. They must have been out of their mind with worry. They thought they were doing their best for their girl.'

Loveday shook her head. 'I can't believe they could withdraw £500,000 from their bank just like that.'

'I doubt if it was that easy. I think Nils Olsen had to call in a few favours from friends.'

'Well, at least they still have their cash,' Loveday said.

Sam sighed. 'I suspect they would give it all up to have their daughter safely home.'

Loveday sat forward. 'I don't understand how you realized the kidnappers would try to snatch the ransom outside the hotel when everything was set up for the drop to be made at the Eden site.'

'It was a hunch. I started wondering why they had been so specific about which hotel the Olsens should book into. They must have known the area, or at least researched it. I could think of only one reason why they would do it.'

'You worked out where they planned to snatch the cash? Very clever,' Loveday said.

'Very clever of them to have totally wrong-footed us. We had about twenty officers up there at Eden – all to no avail.'

'I don't see you could have done it any other way, Sam. You did what you could.'

'It was Cadan who did that. He was amazing the way he launched himself at the motorbike. I was useless. I let the biker escape.'

'Is Cadan all right?'

'A few cuts and scratches,' Sam said. 'He refused medical attention, so we sent him home in a police car. I understand he had to put up with being fussed over by Molly.'

Loveday laughed. The Tremayne's temporary housekeeper was more than capable of keeping Cadan in his place. 'What was Cadan doing there?' she asked.

'He said he'd been on his way to see you at the magazine, but don't ask me why. He never got around to explaining it.'

Loveday shook her head. 'I can't believe all this was going on so close to my office and we knew nothing about it.'

Sam was still deep in thought. 'Cadan knew the Olsens were in Truro. He spotted them coming out of a bank in Boscawen Street and followed them back to their hotel. It was clear something was going on, so we brought the couple in to talk to us. Once they realized we were involved and not going anywhere, they decided to co-operate with us.'

'What about the motorbike? Do you think it could be the one Victor Paton told us about?'

'Possibly. That motorbike is our only clue. You can be sure our people will go over every inch of it. Will you be able to track down the owner?'

'It's listed as stolen,' Sam said. 'But there was a lot of sand in the tyre tread.'

'I don't see how it helps. Cornwall is not exactly short of sandy places.'

'The forensic people are examining tiny seeds found amongst the sand. If they are from plants only found at specific locations it could narrow things down.'

He looked so dejected Loveday got up and put her arms round him. 'Marietta is still alive, Sam. I'm sure of it. You'll find her, like you found Priddy's sketches.'

Sam pulled a face. 'I can't exactly take the credit for that, but we did arrest Billy Travis and he admitted stealing them. Apparently he'd been hanging around the museum trying to figure out how he could burgle the place. His previous attempt had failed miserably, but he hadn't given up. The fire alarm going off was a chance too good to miss. He rushed in when the place was in confusion, grabbed the sketches, zipped them into his jerkin and walked out.'

Loveday slowly shook her head. 'You have to hand it to Billy. He's got some nerve.'

'Pity he doesn't have the brains to go with it,' Sam said, turning Loveday in the direction of the bedroom.

THEY NEEDED no alarm to wake them next morning. Neither of them had slept much. Loveday got up and returned minutes later with mugs of strong coffee. Sam propped himself up on pillows beside her as they sipped their hot drinks in bed and squinted at the dark morning through the gap in the curtains. 'No jogging today?' Sam asked.

'No, I have to get in early. There's a heap of stuff to do before Merrick and Connie get back. Can you believe it's only a week since the wedding?'

'And the Rebecca Monteith murder,' Sam said gloomily. 'We're no further forward with that either.'

Loveday twisted round to look at him. 'You make it sound like it's all your fault.'

'Well, isn't it?'

She gave him a sharp prod in the ribs. 'You know it isn't, so stop beating yourself up. You're not responsible for any of this.' But Loveday knew he was blaming himself for not yet finding Rebecca's killer. And where was Marietta? She knew Sam would not rest until he had an answer to that.

The call came as Sam was about to leave the cottage. Loveday watched his stern expression. 'Yes, Will?' he said sharply. 'What is it?' Her heart gave a lurch as she waited. 'Where?' Sam said. And then, 'I'll be right there.'

He ended the call and turned to her, his eyes solemn. But she already knew what he was going to say.

'It's a body, isn't it?' she said bleakly.

Sam nodded. 'A young woman's body has been found on the beach at Hayle.'

CHAPTER 21

The body was lying amongst the dunes. There had been an attempt to conceal it under sand and reeds, but a black Springer Spaniel had found it. The dog and its shocked owner were waiting in their car for Sam's arrival.

'The body's over here, boss,' Will said, leading the way. He gave a sigh. 'She's naked.'

Sam prepared himself for the sight he didn't want to see, but he forced himself to look. The body was curled into a foetal position, the eyes closed as if in repose. The girl's short cropped hair was the same colour as the wet sandy grave where she lay. Sam gazed down on her and felt his heart tug. She looked so young. Her nakedness only emphasized her vulnerability. He swallowed back the lump in his throat. 'It's not her,' he said. 'It's not Marietta Olsen.'

LOVEDAY'S EYE kept returning to her mobile phone. Sam had promised to call her as soon as they knew more about the body. But when it rang, she drew back. This was it. She was dreading hearing Sam's words. Cadan's face swam before her. He would be devastated if this was Marietta.

Keri was giving her a questioning frown. 'Aren't you going to answer that?'

Loveday reached for her phone and swallowed hard. 'Hello, Sam.'

'It's not Marietta,' he said at once.

The relief that swept over her left her weak. She put a hand to her throat. 'Oh, Sam. Thank God.'

But Sam was in no mood for celebration. 'Don't get too happy, Loveday,' he said. 'We still have a dead girl out there on the dunes, and her family will be equally traumatized.'

'Yes, of course. I'm so sorry, Sam. Is there anything I can do?'

'No, it's fine. I need to contact Cadan before he hears about this on the news and starts to panic.'

'What about the Olsens?'

'A family liaison officer stayed with them last night. She will explain about the discovery of this body. It might not be their daughter, but I don't know how much comfort they will take from that.'

Loveday gave a sad nod. 'We're back to square one, aren't we?' She heard Sam sigh. 'I'm afraid we're even further back now,' he said.

The call had unnerved her. It was a relief the body wasn't Marietta, but Sam was right. This was no time for celebration. She hadn't asked if he thought this grim new discovery could have anything to do with Rebecca's murder, or even the kidnapping of Marietta Olsen.

Loveday tried to imagine what the next police move would be. They would have to identify the dead woman. Would that mean another e-fit? Perhaps they'd found something on the body that might help? Had the body been washed up on the shore? Would the police be able to discover where she went into the sea?

She suddenly realized Sam had only confirmed the body was not Marietta. He'd said nothing more.

'You look like you need one of my special brews.' Keri leaned across the desk.

'No, it's fine, thanks,' Loveday said, reaching for her jacket. 'I need to go out.'

'Where are you going?' Keri called after her.

'Not sure,' Loveday called back as she hurried out of the office. 'I'll let you know.'

She sat downstairs in her car, not sure why she'd made that dramatic exit from the office. She needed to think, and getting out felt like the obvious thing to do. She pulled out her notebook and began to make a list of all the people involved in Sam's case.

Rebecca was at the top of the list. They didn't even know why she'd been killed, let alone who killed her. Loveday tried to picture what the woman's life had been like. If she really had been gay, as Lawrence had suggested, then her life could have been very different from what Loveday had imagined. If she'd had a partner, even a secret one, she didn't think Sam had found her.

Loveday knew of a couple of bars in Penzance and Truro that were frequented by gay and lesbian people. She stopped, frowning, did she also know one in Falmouth? Was the Brush and Pen a gay bar? She was remembering that kiss in the alley between Elise Clark and the distressed young woman.

Now that she thought about it, the pub was exactly the kind of place that might have appealed to Rebecca. She was an artist after all, with strong connections to the Penzance Museum and the Falmouth Art School

Had Sam checked it out? If so, he hadn't mentioned it. She hadn't even told him about her and Cassie's visit there the previous evening. She felt excitement stir in the pit of her stomach and wasn't really sure why.

'Do we know how the girl on the beach died, boss?' DC Alan Rowe asked when the team gathered later for the morning briefing.

'There's no confirmation yet, if that's what you mean. We won't have the post mortem results until the end of the afternoon, but there was an unmistakable stab wound in her chest. It also looked as though there had been an attempt to conceal her body under sand and weeds, but we don't know how much of this the dog dug away.'

'So we have two murders, plus a kidnapping on our hands,' Malcolm Carter said.

Sam gave a grim nod. 'We need to find out why she was naked.'

'Was she sexually abused?' Amanda asked.

'Perhaps,' Sam said. 'We don't know yet, but I don't think so.'

'So her clothes were removed to make it more difficult for us to identify her?' she said.

'That's the more likely reason,' Sam said. 'We'll have an e-fit done after the PM. We do have a clue about the motorbike though. Forensics have analyzed the sand on the tyres and found seeds of wild flowers. The combination of sand and wild flowers narrows down possible sites.' He nodded to Will, who was standing by the whiteboard.

'I've marked the sites we're interested in,' Will said. 'We need to split up and check them out.' Everyone nodded as he allocated teams of two detectives to visit the sites they had identified.

As she sat in the staff car park, Loveday completed her list of the people connected to Rebecca. She then wrote out another list of those who knew Marietta. Having cross-checked, she then drew up a third shorter list of the people she suspected knew both women. Her eyes travelled down what she had written and she gave a sigh. Quite a few had a connection with Falmouth. She pulled a face, staring at the names. She had already decided she would drive to Falmouth before she'd even put the first name on the list.

There was no sign of Elise or her friend when Loveday walked into the bar. It was a lot quieter than when she'd been here with Cassie. She climbed onto one of the bar stools and smiled at the barman. 'Can I have a white wine spritzer, please?'

She watched him top up the small measure of wine with soda water and looked around her.

'Didn't I see you here last night?' he asked as he passed the glass across the bar.

Loveday nodded. 'The place was so busy I'm surprised you noticed me.'

'We always notice our new customers,' he said, his eyes taking in her smart grey trouser suit. 'Forgive me for saying, but you don't have the look of a penniless artist.'

'I'm not an artist.' She laughed. 'But many of my friends are and I'd heard so much about this place that I had to see it for myself.'

'And here you are again,' the barman said. 'Does that mean we met with your approval?'

'Definitely,' Loveday said, her eye going to the collection of photos pinned to the back wall.

'Our rogue's gallery,' the barman said. 'The regulars compete with each other to get their picture up there.'

'They all look like they're having a great time,' Loveday said, scanning the faces for any sign of Rebecca, but she wasn't there. Marietta was though. She had her arms around Cadan and they appeared to be singing. And then she spotted Elise.

'I know this woman.' She pointed to the photo of the barmaid and the customer Loveday had seen her kissing. 'Wasn't she working here last night?'

'That's Elise – and I don't fancy being here when she sees it.'

'Why not?' Loveday asked.

'Elise is almost paranoid about having her photo taken. Another member of staff took this for a joke last night and stuck it on the wall behind her back. Elise will go spare when she sees it, but I'm not getting involved.'

'Who is that she's with in the photo?'

'I don't know. She's not a regular but I've seen her in here a few times.'

A customer at the other end of the bar caught his attention and he went off to serve him. Loveday slipped her hand into her bag and drew out her phone. She waited until she was sure no one was looking before zooming in on the photo and snapping a picture of it. She had a feeling this picture could be important, although just at that moment she had no idea why.

It was almost 2 o'clock when she got back to Truro and her phone buzzed alerting her to a new text message. It was from Sam.

'Have you eaten yet? How about meeting me in five minutes for a quick pasty and pint in the Crab and Creel? xx'

'Perfect xx,' she texted back.

He was already there when Loveday walked in. She could tell by his expression things weren't going well.

'I take it you haven't any more news about Marietta?'

'No, not yet.'

'What about this morning's body?'

'Same thing.' Sam shook his head. 'Whoever put her there made a good job of stripping her of every shred of identity. We've given the media an e-fit, but it hasn't made the news yet.'

'And the motorbike?' Loveday asked.

'It was stolen. We've traced the owner. He's a fifty-five-year-old skinhead from Plymouth. He reported the bike stolen a month ago. We don't believe he has anything to do with the kidnapping.' He took a mouthful of pasty and wiped the crumbs from his mouth.

'Forensics got us excited about traces of wildflower seeds they found on the tyres. We're ongoing with searches of sites they could have come from.' He put the pasty back on his plate and sighed. 'Will and I are going over to check out Crantock this afternoon, but to be honest, we don't even know what we're looking for.'

Loveday drained the last of the pot of tea she'd ordered. 'I wish I could help,' she said. 'You'd tell me if there was anything I could do, wouldn't you, Sam?'

Sam tilted his head affectionately at her. 'There's definitely nothing you can do, Loveday, but thanks for the offer.'

'Cassie and I were in that pub in Falmouth.' She paused. 'You know, the one Cadan and Marietta go to.'

Sam raised an eyebrow. 'You didn't mention it.'

'Sorry, I forgot. Anyway I didn't discover anything useful.' She bit her lip. 'Unless…'

'Unless what?'

'You've interviewed that flatmate of hers a couple of times.'

Sam nodded. 'Elise Clark, yes, why?'

'Did you get any impression of her being gay?'

'No, I doubt if she is. If anything I'd say she's probably a bit of a man eater. What makes you think she's gay?'

'I saw her kissing someone…another woman. But now I'm wondering if I read too much into it.'

'Probably,' Sam said, looking at his watch. 'You must excuse me, Loveday. I have to go. I told Will I'd meet him ten minutes ago.'

Loveday held her face up to be kissed. 'Will you let me know if you get any more news of Marietta?'

'I promise,' Sam said, snatching up the half-eaten pasty as he hurried off.

WILL LOOKED up and glanced at the clock as Sam put his head

round the door of the incident room. 'Sorry to keep you waiting, Will. Are we good to go?'

'Yes.' Will grabbed his jacket and chased after his senior officer.

'I don't suppose anything new came in while I was away?'

'Nothing,' Will said. 'In fact I think this whole wildflower thing is a waste of time.'

'Have you a better idea?' Sam asked.

'No, but I really don't see the point in searching beaches. So what if the biker visited a beach. It doesn't tell us anything.'

'Agreed, but there's a chance it might lead us to where the biker lives.'

Will pulled a face. 'I think we're clutching at straws.'

It was still daylight when they arrived at Crantock beach, but judging by the dark clouds Sam could see rolling in, that wouldn't last long. The detectives got out of their car and scanned the beach.

'You have a wander along there, Will. I'll go the other way. If we don't find anything in the next half hour, we'll call it a day.'

Will screwed up his eyes. 'Is that a caravan site up there?'

Sam followed his gaze. From where he stood on the lower level of the beach he could make out the flat roofs of two caravans.

'You said we were looking for somewhere this biker might be holed up,' Will said, but Sam was already scrambling up the bank. 'Forget the beach search,' he said. 'This looks much more promising.'

They had knocked on the doors of ten caravans before a harassed middle-aged woman told them about a motorbike owner on the far side of the site. 'Always kicking up a racket roaring about the place on that thing. If you're here to arrest them then you've got my blessing.' She pointed to the far row of caravans. 'I don't know which one they've got, but it's one of them.'

Sam was beginning to feel a tiny jab of hope. They got no response to two of the doors they tried, but the third one opened sharply at their repeated knocking and an elderly man stood blinking at them. 'What d'ye want?' he snapped. 'You'd better have a good excuse for battering down my door when I'm having a kip.'

Sam and Will produced their warrant cards. The man looked even less impressed. 'We're looking for one of your neighbours,' Sam said. 'One who rides a motorbike.'

'Oh, her. What d'ye want with her?'

'The biker is a woman?'

'Isn't that what I said? But she's not here. I haven't seen her all day.'

'Which one is her caravan?' Will asked.

The man nodded next door.

'I don't see any motorbike,' Sam said, watching the man.

'Nor have I, not since she went storming out of here this morning.' He scratched his head. 'Or was that yesterday?'

'How long has your neighbour had this motorbike?'

'I've no idea. She only moved in about a month ago.'

Sam and Will exchanged a look.

'I don't suppose you have a key to your neighbour's caravan?' Sam said.

'No need. She keeps a spare under that big stone by the step.'

Sam told the man to return to his caravan. He didn't want an audience when he and Will checked out the biker's caravan.

It was a lot neater inside than they had expected. There was no pile of dirty dishes in the sink. The bed was unmade but there were no clothes strewn untidily about the place.

Sam checked the drawers. He found a bank statement for a Christine Stowe. She was in the red by almost £1,000. There was a black leather jerkin in the wardrobe.

Will opened the fridge door. 'Looks like she needs to do a food shop. There's only a tub of margarine and two eggs in here.'

'Have you noticed something?' Sam looked round. 'No photographs, and I couldn't see a family album anywhere.'

'It's almost like she doesn't live here,' Will said. 'Like it's somewhere to doss down, but not to live in.' He turned to Sam. 'D'you think this is our kidnapper?'

'That's a bit of a leap,' Sam said. 'The only link forensics have given us to this place is a plant.'

'And a motor bike,' Will said.

Sam sighed. 'I suppose we have to start somewhere.' He went outside and rang for back-up. 'And get a scene of crime team out here,' he said, staring at the tyre tracks in the mud at the rear end of the caravan.

IT WAS after 10 o'clock when Sam got home to Marazion. He had kept Loveday informed about what was happening at the caravan site and she'd waited up for him.

'Well?' she said excitedly, going to meet him as he came through the door. 'Have you found our biker?'

'Not exactly,' Sam said, collapsing into a chair. 'But we think we may have found where she was staying.'

'And I don't suppose there was any sign of Marietta there?'

Sam shook his head. 'None. I feel we're taking one step forward and two back.'

'Of course you're not. You and Will did brilliantly finding that caravan site. It's bound to lead to clues about where this woman is and when you find her you'll find Marietta. I know it.'

'I'm still thinking of that poor woman on the beach this morning. We've had no positive response to the e-fit, which makes me think she's not from this area.'

'Or maybe the majority of people simply haven't seen it,' Loveday said. 'I haven't turned on the TV today, so I haven't seen the e-fit.'

'Take a look if you like,' Sam said wearily. 'It's in my coat pocket.'

Loveday went to where Sam had hung his coat and fished the new e-fit picture out of his pocket. She stared at it, frowning and then her fingers went to her temple. 'Oh my God, Sam. I think I know her.'

CHAPTER 22

Loveday tapped her mobile phone to bring up the picture of the two women she'd snapped in the pub. 'Is she your body on the dunes?'

Sam took the phone and his eyes widened. 'Where did you get this?'

'I took it. That was one of the pictures on the wall of the Brush and Pen. They call it their rogues gallery.'

She perched on the arm of Sam's chair, looking over his shoulder at the image on her phone. 'The other one is Marietta's flatmate, isn't she?'

'Yes, that's Elise.' But his attention was on the younger woman. 'I don't suppose you know who she is?'

'No idea,' Loveday said, 'but she's the one who was in the bar last night when Cassie and I were there, the one I told you I saw Elise kissing. But that was after what had looked like a row. The other woman had definitely not been happy.'

'Really?' Sam said, his brows coming together like he was trying to work something out. 'In what way not happy?'

'I can't be sure, but it looked like she was having a go at Elise.'

Sam stared at the photo. 'I'll send this to the incident room and we need to speak to Elise again.'

Loveday glanced at the clock. 'She'll still be working at the pub, the barman said she was on duty tonight.' She couldn't ignore the curious look Sam was giving her. 'OK, I hold my hands up. I went back to there this morning.'

'Why?'

'Cadan told me Marietta took him there. I just felt there was a connection between this pub and all the other things going on. That's why I took the photo.'

'Was it the only reason?'

'The barman told me a member of staff had taken the picture the previous evening and stuck it up behind the bar after Elise had finished her shift. He said she would be furious when she saw it.'

'Why did he think that?'

'Apparently Elise likes her privacy. The photo was put up to provoke her.'

'You said you thought these two women were having a row?'

'It looked more like the one with the cropped hair was having a go at Elise. She was certainly agitated about something. I think Elise was trying to pacify her.'

Loveday wasn't sure if Sam was regarding this as an important piece of information or a reason to chastise her for getting over-involved in his case again. She waited, going over everything in her head, making sure she got her words right. 'I saw Elise lifting the bar hatch and ushering the other woman through.' She flashed Sam a defensive glance. 'OK, so I was curious. I admit it. I went outside and slipped into the alley at the side of the pub, where the empty beer crates are kept.'

'And!' Sam was getting impatient.

'The back door of the pub opened and the pair came out. The agitated one was in tears. Elise put her arms around her.' She paused. 'That's when I saw them kissing.'

'And this why you asked if there was any indication Elise is gay?'

Loveday nodded. She put up a hand. 'Wait a minute. I've remembered something else.' Loveday's mind was scrolling back to the previous evening when she'd watched the two women leave the bar. 'She was limping,' she said.

'Who? Elise?' Sam said.

'No, the other one. She definitely looked like she was limping.'

He got up and punched a number into his phone. She heard him give instructions to find Elise.

It seemed wrong to be doing anything as normal as going to bed that night when so much else was going on. She knew neither of them would sleep. And she'd been right. As soon Sam's mobile buzzed an hour later she could tell by how quickly he'd grabbed it that he was wide awake. He'd been waiting for the call.

'What is it? What's happening?' Loveday said, rolling over and perching herself up on her elbow. She could hear the urgency in Sam's voice. 'We need to find her. Drop everything else if need be, this is the priority. And get someone back out to that caravan site in Crantock. If it means knocking up every single resident to find Elise Clark then do it.' He ended the call, tossed back the duvet and sprang out of bed.

'You're not going into the station?' Loveday said, dismayed. 'You've only just got to bed, Sam. Let your team deal with this.'

'They can't find Elise,' he said, rifling through his drawer for a clean shirt. 'She didn't turn up for her shift tonight and she's not at home.'

Loveday's head was spinning as she watched Sam scrambling into his clothes. 'Are you going back to Crantock?' she asked. 'D'you think that woman in my photo could have lived there?'

'We don't know. At the moment we're pitching straws into the wind, but we have to identify the murder victim from the dunes.'

An uneasy feeling was beginning to creep over Loveday. 'You're going to ask me to make that identification, aren't you?'

'From your memory of seeing a woman only briefly in a pub? That would be a last resort,' Sam said. 'The bar staff would know her better. We also need to find out if they ever saw her dressed in bikers' leathers.'

Loveday stared at the door for some time after Sam had gone, trying to sort out the thoughts racing through her head. She tried to picture the scene between the two women in the pub again. It hadn't exactly been a row. It had looked more like Elise's girlfriend have been accusing her of something. Blaming her for something bad that had happened perhaps? But what? It had been difficult to work out Elise's reaction. She'd clearly been trying to placate the young woman at the same time as coping with the demands of the pub customers.

If this was the woman in the e-fit, did Elise now know that her friend – who was possibly her lover – was dead? But how could she know? Had Elise witnessed the woman being killed? Had she discovered the body and panicked? Loveday's heart missed a beat. Her head sunk back onto the pillow. She'd thought of something else. Had Elise Clark killed her lover?

Sam had called everyone together for an early team briefing. He had the feeling they were on the verge of a major breakthrough, but was it the one that would lead them to finding Marietta Olsen? Enough mistakes had been made, they couldn't afford any more. He had a feeling most of the jigsaw pieces were already on the table. The tricky thing now was figuring out how to assemble them.

'We have a witness who has suggested the body on the dunes

has a connection to Elise Clark – Marietta's landlady.' The team had arrived bleary-eyed from their previous late-night working. Now eyebrows were shooting up around the room.

'What sort of connection, sir?' Amanda Fox asked.

'If the witness has correctly identified the victim from the e-fit then she was seen with Elise at the Brush and Pen pub in Falmouth, where Elise works.'

Amanda screwed up her face. 'What does this have to do with the Crantock caravan site? Even if we establish this is the base for the biker who tried to snatch the ransom cash I don't see what it has to do with our victim.'

Sam's eyes went around the group. 'DC Fox is right, everyone. We can't make assumptions, so we have work to do.' He nodded to Will. 'Any word yet from Dr Bartholomew?'

'Not as much as we'd like. Apparently they have a backlog of post mortems to do down at the morgue. So what information he's given us so far will only be half the story.' Sam raised an eyebrow. 'Yeah, I know.' Will grimaced. 'But that's what he said. What he has been able say though is that the victim was stabbed with a long-handled knife.' He glanced up. 'And we know Rebecca Monteith was stabbed by a similar weapon. This latest victim also had bruising along her left side, but the pathologist could offer no definite explanation.'

'Could it be the kind of bruising a person might get by being hurled off a motorbike at speed?' DC Malcolm Carter asked.

'I asked that,' Will said. 'Dr Bartholomew wasn't prepared to commit himself without further examination of the body, but he agreed it was a possibility.'

Malcolm Carter unfolded his arms and sat forward. 'So our biker and our victim might be the same person?'

'It's something we'll be looking at,' Sam said.

Amanda was nodding thoughtfully. 'If we have a witness who saw the victim talking to Elise then could she also be implicated in the kidnapping?'

'This is what we're considering,' Sam said gravely. 'Which is why it's imperative we find Elise. If we're right, she could lead us to Marietta.'

DC Alan Rowe put up a hand. 'Going back to what DS Tregellis said, if the latest victim was stabbed with a long-bladed knife, same as the first one. Does this mean we believe it's the same killer?'

'It's possible, Alan,' Sam said. 'We need to take the caravan in Crantock apart. I know it's already been searched and nothing's been found, but we need to go over it again inch by inch. And we need to speak to the residents, in particular the man in the neighbouring caravan. I have a feeling he knows more than he's told us.' He swivelled back to the whiteboard. 'We've applied for a warrant to search Elise Clark's flat and as soon as the Brush and Pen opens we need to find a member of staff who can identify our victim.'

They all looked up as the door to the incident room opened and a young dark-haired female officer came smartly in. 'This call has just come in, sir,' she said, handing Sam a note. 'The sergeant thought you should have it straight away.'

Sam read the note and his head came up. 'It seems we have another witness who claims our victim is a Chrissie Stowe. She's a parcel courier, drives an old Ford van – and has a passion for Harley Davidson motorbikes.' A buzz of excitement went round the room. 'According to this witness,' Sam continued. 'The victim was also a leading light in the gay pride movement in Newquay.' He gave a grim smile. 'I'll check this one out myself. The rest of you have your instructions. You know what you have do. Let's get this show back on the road, people.'

He looked at Will. 'You're with me, Will. We're going to Newquay.'

MERIDIAN CLOSE WAS a group of austere looking former council houses at the top end of Newquay. Sam was surprised at how close the place was to Crantock. Surely the woman wouldn't have hired a caravan if she had a house here? But then she would probably have been known in the area, whereas she could be more or less anonymous on the caravan site.

'It's number 51,' Sam said. 'The house on the corner.'

They went up the path and knocked, with no expectation of anyone answering. A head appeared from over the privet hedge that divided the gardens of the two semi-detached houses. 'She's not in. Can I be of any help?' the woman said, her gaze flitting expectantly from one officer to the other.

The detectives produced their ID cards and the woman nodded. 'Yes, I thought that's who you were.' They could hear the excitement in her voice. 'It was me who rang you. I saw that picture on *Spotlight* last night. It's her, isn't it? It's Chrissie.'

Sam gave the woman an interested smile. 'Could we have a word, Mrs...' His voice rose questioningly.

'It's Melbourne,' the woman said quickly. 'Sandra Melbourne and yes, please come round.'

Sam and Will found their way around the dense hedge. It reminded him of the hedge, which bordered his and Loveday's rambling front garden in Marazion. Apart from keeping the grass to a manageable level they more or less left it to its own devices. The wild rabbits liked it that way and he and Loveday had no objections.

There was no sign of any rabbits at 53, Meridian Close, only a fussing old lady who appeared to be enjoying the drama of this.

Sandra Melbourne's short brown wavy hair was caught back from her face with grips. They followed her into a busy front room. Sam had never seen so many ornaments, but the woman obviously treasured them because there wasn't a speck of dust anywhere. She settled herself into an armchair and indicated the two detectives should also sit. They did. 'Now,' she said, a bit breathlessly. 'What's this all about? Is Chrissie OK?'

'How long have you known your neighbour?' Sam asked.

Sandra frowned at them. 'I've always known her. Chrissie grew up next door. It was her parents' house. Mind you, she's not here a lot of the time, which is a good thing because that motorbike of hers makes such a racket.'

'When did you last see Chrissie, Mrs Melbourne?' Sam asked.

'Sandra, please. Call me Sandra.' Her eyes went to the ceiling as she tried to remember. 'Must be about a week. I thought it was odd because she didn't take her motorbike.'

'Are you sure?' Sam said.

'Take a look for yourself. It's out the back there, under its tarpaulin.' She eyed them suspiciously. 'What's happened to her? Why are you looking for her?'

Sam met her eyes. 'It's bad news, I'm afraid. There was a body found on the beach at Hayle yesterday.'

Sandra Melbourne put a hand to her face. 'It's not Chrissie, is it?'

'We haven't found anyone to officially identify her yet,' Sam said quietly.

'I'll do it,' the woman said. 'I won't rest until I know if it's her. When would you like me to come?'

CHAPTER 23

Marietta's voice was hoarse from shouting. She knew they were there. She could hear them moving around. Why didn't they come? They hadn't brought her bag of food either. When the biker didn't come, Marietta prayed it was because they were going to free her. But that was days ago and they still hadn't come. How many days? She looked at her fingers trying to count, but it was hopeless.

They had given her blankets and she huddled in a corner, wrapping them around herself. Why were they doing this? Were they expecting her parents to pay for her release? Or was her imprisonment some kind of punishment? She screwed her eyes tight shut, trying to clear her mind. Is that why Rebecca had been killed? Was someone punishing her? But for what? Rebecca had been one of the kindest people she'd ever met. She'd had endless patience with her at college when they discussed her work. Not many people understood her. She was unaware of the wistful smile curving her mouth as she remembered the kindly woman.

Marietta forced herself to her feet, taking the blankets with her as she paced around the room. Surely people were looking for her? Cadan would definitely be trying to find her. She frowned. He would, wouldn't he?

In her mind's eye she could feel his touch, his fingers stroking her face, her hair. She could feel his mouth on hers when he kissed her. She knew Cadan had his enemies, sometimes he deserved not to be liked, but he had always treated her well. Sometimes she fancied he loved her. She took a long shuddering breath. Where was he now?

'I NEED YOUR HELP, LOVEDAY,' Cadan said as soon as she picked up the phone. 'Something's going on and I need your advice. Can we meet?'

The urgency in his voice was striking alarm bells in Loveday's head. She felt protective of Cadan because he was Merrick's half-brother, but he did get himself into some pretty rough scrapes. She rolled her eyes to the ceiling. 'Please tell me you're not up to something dodgy, Cadan.'

He gave an exasperated sigh. 'I'll pretend you didn't say that.'

'OK, sorry,' Loveday said. 'What is this something?'

'I don't want to talk about it on the phone. I'm in Penzance. Is there any chance you can join me?'

She hesitated. 'You want me to meet you in Penzance? But why? Just tell me what's going on.'

'I can't, you'll have to trust me,' he said. 'Please tell me you'll come.'

The last time Cadan came looking for her was because Marietta had disappeared and he couldn't make anyone believe something serious had happened to her, that was days ago and Marietta was still missing.

'OK. I'll come. Where are you?'

'Do you know the auctioneers place in Alverton?'

'Well yes, but…'

He cut her off. 'I'll wait there in the car park,' he said.

'I'm still at the office, Cadan. It'll take an hour or so to drive down.'

'That's fine. Come as soon as you can.'

Loveday could imagine a dozen different scams Cadan could have got himself involved with. Was he now in trouble with the police and wanting her help to get away?

She wouldn't put anything past him. Her mobile phone rang again. It was Sam. 'Don't bother cooking for me tonight, Loveday,' he said. 'I've no idea when I'll get home.'

'Any more news of Marietta?' she asked. It was becoming a regular mantra.

She heard him heave a sigh. 'Not yet, but we've identified the body at Hayle. Does the name Chrissie Stowe mean anything to you?'

Loveday screwed up her forehead, thinking. 'No, sorry, Sam.'

'Never mind. It was only a thought. Don't do anything I wouldn't do tonight, will you?'

'As if I would.' Loveday laughed. She frowned at the phone for a few seconds after the call had ended. Should she have told Sam about Cadan's call? But what could she have said? She didn't know herself what it was about…not yet.

Cadan must have been watching for her because he came striding across the car park as soon as she turned off the road. He waited until she had pulled into a space before going forward to open the passenger door and climbed in beside her.

Loveday arched an eyebrow. 'What's this all about, Cadan?'

His face glowed with excitement. 'She's alive, Loveday. Marietta is alive!'

Loveday's heart quickened. 'How do you know? Have you seen her?'

'No.' He turned towards her, his brow creasing as though trying to find the most convincing way of telling it. 'I went to see the Olsens,' he explained. 'Did you know they hold me responsible for Marietta's abduction? They never liked me, but to accuse me of that…'

'Can we get back to the point?' Loveday said.

Cadan pushed his hand through his hair and she noticed he was shaking. 'I was going to see the Olsens to ask if they'd heard anything new about Marietta.' He slanted a look at her. 'Well, your Sam isn't doing anything to find her.'

'He's doing what he can,' Loveday said.

'Oh yeah? But it was me who had to step in when it was all kicking off outside the Olsens' hotel. If I hadn't thrown myself at the biker they would have got away with the ransom cash.' Cadan's face stretched into an angry frown. 'And if Sam and his woodentops hadn't let them escape we might already have Marietta back with us.'

Loveday knew how bad Sam felt about that, but it was hardly his fault when the kidnappers had done such a brilliant job of setting them up.

'Nobody's disputing you did well,' she said sharply. 'Can you get to the point now?'

'Well, it was like I said. I went to see the Olsens in their hotel. I knew the room number, so I skipped past reception and went upstairs.'

Loveday waited, wondering when he would get to the bit about Marietta being alive.

He continued. 'I was about to knock when I heard a mobile phone ringing on the other side of the door and then Giselle's voice answering it. She sounded strange, like she'd been expecting the call and dreading it at the same time. My heart sank. I thought she was being told Marietta was… Well, I thought it was bad news.'

'Go on,' Loveday said, her eyes glued to his face.

Cadan swallowed. 'Then I heard Giselle demanding proof that Marietta was alive. She'd hit the speaker on the phone, presumably so Nils could listen too. Anyway, suddenly I could hear this strange, aggressive voice barking instructions at them.' He paused. 'It was them! The kidnappers. I couldn't stop shaking. I was terrified one of the hotel staff would come and make a fuss about why I was loitering there when I wasn't even staying at the place.' He swallowed.

'I kept my ear to the door and heard the caller say, *"Look at the picture, I've sent you, Mrs Olsen. That's your girl and you'll see from the date she's holding up today's Western Morning News."'*

He looked up and met Loveday's eyes. 'The kidnappers are having another go at getting that ransom.'

Loveday stared back at him, her heart quickening. 'Are you sure?'

'Of course I'm sure. I heard them, didn't I?'

'Tell me exactly what you heard, Cadan, exactly what was said.'

'I put it on my phone, but the recording's not great. Listen!'

Loveday cocked her head, concentrating on the burred recording. The voice sounded harsh and fragmented. She had no doubt it had been doctored so it couldn't be identified. She thought she could make out:

'Put the cash in a secure plastic bag. Leave the hotel car park at exactly 2pm and drive to Penzance. At that time of day it should take no more than 1hr 10 mins.

In Chapel Street there's a pub called the Admiral Benbow. Go in at exactly 3.30pm. Order a drink and sit at the table by the window to right of door. Your ongoing instructions are in an envelope stuck to the underside of the table.'

Loveday checked her watch. It was 2 o'clock. 'We need to call Sam.'

Cadan drew back as though he'd been stung. 'That's the last thing we're going to do. Have you forgotten what happened last time? We've got another chance to save Marietta. I'm keeping the police well out of it.'

Loveday shook her head. 'You can't do this on your own, Cadan.'

'But I'm not on my own, am I? You're here.'

Despite herself Loveday couldn't help laughing at the man's audacity. 'You know I'll have to tell Sam about this.'

Cadan gave a reluctant nod. 'All I'm asking is that you wait until we have more information. We've no idea where the ransom drop is going to be yet. When we know that then we'll both call Sam. I don't want the police involved, not yet. We don't want the whole thing going pear-shaped again.'

Loveday pushed her fingers through her hair. How could she have allowed herself to get involved in this? She was trying not to imagine Sam's face when he found out. But there was some sense in what Cadan had said. They didn't know where the ransom drop was to be made. She bit her bottom lip, thinking. 'OK, Cadan,' she said. 'What do you want to do?'

'I think we should get to the Admiral Benbow and find a parking place from where we can watch who is coming and going.'

'Won't the kidnappers see us?'

He pressed his lips together and nodded. 'I'm hoping they will be more desperate this time and make mistakes. I doubt if there's been time to organize this properly. They'll be all over the place.'

Loveday's heart was beginning to thud. If Cadan was right, where did that leave Marietta?

'We'll take your car if that's OK, Loveday. My little sports car is too conspicuous.'

Loveday nodded and put the car into gear. She had a sick feeling in the pit of her stomach as they drove back through the town and turned down into Chapel Street. She was looking ahead down the hill trying to spot a parking place.

'The Admiral Benbow is near the bottom on the left,' Cadan said.

'Yes, I know. I'm looking for a place to park.'

'There's a space on the right, look, where the car's just pulling out.'

'I see it,' Loveday said, manoeuvring the Clio into the vacated space. She turned off the engine, looking across at the pub. 'What now?'

'We wait,' Cadan said. 'The Olsens' instructions were to enter the pub at exactly 3.30. That's an hour away. Even if the kidnappers turn up to keep watch and make sure the Olsens follow instructions I doubt if they will be here yet.'

It was half an hour before the car turned up. Cadan watched its approach in the wing mirror. 'I think we have company,' he said.

He slumped down in the seat as it passed and parked on the other side of the road ahead. 'I don't believe it,' he said. 'Not her!'

Loveday was swallowing a lump in her throat. She had also recognized the driver. It was Elise Clark.

Cadan and Loveday shrank back in their seats. 'What's she doing here?' she whispered. But she needed no reply. There could be only one reason why the woman was here. She was the one who had arranged this. Elise Clark was Marietta's kidnapper!

CHAPTER 24

Elise Clark was still trying to get her head around what she was doing. It was too easy. Her hand shook as she raised it to the mirror. It was half an hour before Nils Olsen was due. She was being given a second chance. If this was to work she had to keep a lid on her feelings. Things had seemed so different that morning.

In her mind's eye she was back in the filthy ruin, crouching in the gloom below the barricaded windows. The knife was on the floor beside her. She couldn't stop pictures racing through her mind, blood red pictures that were spiralling out of control. She'd clutched at her head, violently rocking it, but the pictures had still been there. She had to get rid of them, to clear her mind. She had to think!

The girl's relentless whimpering and banging on the walls had gone on and on. Elise was reaching the end of her wits. 'Shut up,' she'd yelled as the battering and whining got louder. 'Shut up! Shut up!' But the relentless screaming hadn't stopped. It had jangled through her head to the point of agony.

Her eye had gone to the knife. It still had Chrissie's blood on it. Sweet, stupid Chrissie. Why could she not have done what she'd been told? It would all have worked out if only Chrissie hadn't been so weak.

She'd squeezed her eyes tight shut trying to escape the images flashing through her head. That look of disbelief in Chrissie's eyes as she plunged the knife into her chest would be with her forever.

Elise hadn't been aware of the tears that had stained her cheeks, she'd only known she had to pull herself together. The knife had still been on the floor beside her. She'd kicked it into a corner. She hadn't been able to think straight while it was there, glinting up at her.

Her mind had been going over the ransom snatch again. She'd tortured herself about how her meticulous planning had gone so disastrously wrong. How had that happened? The Olsens had clearly gone to the police, but she had expected it. It's why she'd set up the decoy ransom drop at the Eden site. She'd been trying not to think how freaked out Chrissie had been when it all went wrong.

She'd come to the pub that night in total panic mode. Elise could still see her sitting at the bar, begging her to walk off her shift. They needed to talk, she'd said.

Elise shook her head. Poor Chrissie. She'd been full of remorse. The bag containing the ransom money had been in her hand when the man had appeared from nowhere and launched himself at her. She'd come flying off the motorbike, landing painfully on her side. She'd insisted there was no way she could have saved the money. Her only thought had been to get herself out of there.

Chrissie had explained she'd been vaguely aware of the chaos she'd left behind her in the road as she'd fled. A man had chased after her, but she'd been too quick for him and had escaped into the busy street of shoppers, ducking into a book shop and staying there until she'd felt it was safe to leave.

Elise heaved a deep sigh just thinking about it. She'd planned it all so meticulously well and Chrissie had let her down. She was imagining the bag of money bursting open when Chrissie let go of it. The thought of those hundred-pound notes fluttering down Lemon Street when they should have been safely stashed away in the bag in the cottage as they'd planned was unbearable. Chrissie had to be punished. She'd had to be silenced!

Elise's eye had kept straying back to where the knife lay. Killing became easier the more often you did it.

It had always been her plan to kill Marietta Olsen. She could identify her. But that didn't matter. It was the girl's incessant whining and her constant whimpering to be set free that wound Elise up the most.

She'd been reaching for the knife when the idea came to her. The Olsens already had the money. If she could convince them Marietta was still alive, and they could have her back if they paid the ransom she might still be able to rescue this disaster.

Elise had rifled through her bag for the copy of that morning's *Western Morning News*. She'd bought it to read what they had written about Chrissie, but there had been nothing. Maybe it had been a news item on the radio or TV?

The paper could still serve its purpose though. She'd grabbed it and marched through to the room where she was holding Marietta. A picture of the girl holding up the newspaper, with the date very visible, would be proof positive for the Olsens that their daughter was alive.

They'd been willing to pay the ransom before, and they would be even more desperate now. They were putty in her hands. The police had let them down. The Olsens wouldn't be giving them a second chance.

Excitement tingled through her as she sat in her car outside the Admiral Benbow. She knew she could still make this work. Her eyes were fixed on the mirror, waiting for the first confirmation that Nils Olsen was carrying out her instructions.

Loveday could see Cadan's hands clenched into fists as he stared at Elise's car. 'It was her, wasn't it?' he said. 'All this time we've been searching for Marietta, and the one who took her was right here under our noses.'

Loveday laid her hand on his fists and felt the tension there. She could tell he was struggling to stop himself from charging across the road and grabbing the woman by the throat. 'Try to keep calm, Cadan,' she said. 'We have to stay with this.'

He was shaking his head, his eyes still fixed on Elise's car. 'She was supposed to be Marietta's friend. She trusted her, for God's sake. We both did. What kind of evil bitch does something like this?'

'Look,' Loveday said. 'It's Olsen, he's here.

Cadan swallowed. 'Should one of us follow him into the pub?'

'No.' Loveday was firm. 'We'll wait. Elise hasn't left her car. Let's wait and see what happens.' She forced a smile. 'We have to concentrate on staying calm.'

A few minutes later Nils Olsen appeared at the pub door. 'He's coming back,' Loveday said. The man was clutching an envelope and was striding back to his car. He took off within seconds, Elise close behind him. Loveday started the engine and followed them at a distance, being careful not to be spotted. She could see Cadan tensing beside her. 'We're going to lose them,' he said, his voice rising. 'Get closer.'

'Trust me,' Loveday said. 'We're not going to lose them.' But she was worried at the speed all this was happening. She still hadn't contacted Sam.

Ahead she could see Nils negotiating his way out of Chapel Street to the seafront. He turned left along Wharf Road with Elise behind him.

'What are they playing at?' Cadan snapped. 'Are they going back to Truro? Maybe Nils has already made the drop? Maybe he left it somewhere on the way to Penzance and all this is an elaborate subterfuge.'

'I don't think so,' Loveday said. 'Elise wouldn't still be following Nils. My guess is she will grab the ransom at her first chance and hightail it out of here.'

Cadan was biting his nails. 'I don't trust this woman. Once she's got the cash she won't care about Marietta. And if Marietta could identify her then…'

'Let's concentrate on finding your girlfriend,' Loveday said, her eyes on the two vehicles ahead.

Without warning, Elise suddenly made a left turn while Nils carried on.

'What's happening? Where's she going?' Cadan said, his body straining forward.

Loveday had to make a split-second decision which one to follow. She turned left after Elise.

'Why have you done this?' Cadan demanded. 'I thought we were following the ransom.'

'I figure Elise knows where the drop will be made since she's running the show,' Loveday said, hoping she sounded more confident than she felt. She had no idea where this was going, but she was trying to put herself in Elise's place.

The first attempt to get the ransom failed disastrously. Her accomplice, Chrissie Stowe was dead, possibly murdered by Elise herself. She might also have killed Rebecca Monteith. She had nothing to lose. One final audacious attempt to get her hands on that ransom would surely make perfect sense to Elise.

Loveday tried to clear her head. 'Let's try to work out what's going on here,' she said. 'I've been on this road scores of times. It's a shortcut to St Ives. What if the spot for the ransom drop is somewhere off this road?'

Cadan's look suggested he thought she could have lost her mind.

'Work with me on this, Cadan. Elise will be sure by now that the Olsens haven't contacted the police. She'll be feeling confident, maybe over-confident. What if she's on the direct road to the drop point! She'll want to be there before Nils, so she sends him off on the longer route.'

'I'm not sure,' Cadan said. 'That's all supposition.'

'Of course it is.' Loveday nodded. 'I'm trying to think like she might. If I'm right then Nils has been instructed to take the road that bypasses Carbis Bay to St Ives. If he turns off in the centre of the town and heads for the road towards Zennor then he and Elise could cross paths.'

Cadan screwed up his face. 'Sounds a bit far-fetched to me.'

'Well, let's just see,' Loveday said, focusing on Elise's car, two vehicles ahead.

They drove through Nancledra and carried on past the pub at Cripplesease. Loveday was now sure they were on their way to St Ives when she saw Elise make a left turn. She braked, travelling at a crawl to the turning. The signpost indicated a caravan and campsite. Was this to be the drop point?

Loveday waited until Elise's car was out of sight around a corner. It was getting dark now. Elise had turned her lights on. If Loveday did that they would almost certainly be discovered. She would have to rely on the beam from the woman's lights ahead to keep on following her.

'I don't like the look of this,' Cadan said. 'I think she knows we're following her and she's taking us on a wild goose chase.'

The logic wasn't lost on Loveday, but they were committed now. They had passed the turning for the campsite and were continuing along the twisting single-track road deep into the countryside. She was aware of the looks Cadan was sliding in her direction and was beginning to agree she'd made a wrong call when she saw the beam of Elise's car lights veer off to the left. She had turned off the road and was continuing to drive. The moon had come out, so they were not in total darkness. Loveday drove slowly on, trying to assess where Elise could have turned off, when she saw the sign.

'I know where we are!' She swung round to Cadan. 'It's

Towednack Church. I've been here before. We carried a feature in the magazine about a group of ladies who were researching the names on some of the ancient gravestones.'

'Really?' Cadan said, clearly not impressed. 'So why has Elise brought us here?'

'Well, the road she's pulled into only goes to the church. I think this is the drop point,' Loveday said, driving further ahead until she found a farm gate to pull in beside.

'We'll go back on foot, but we have to keep quiet.'

Cadan nodded. Loveday could tell he was getting more engaged with this. 'Look!' She pointed ahead. 'It's her car. She's tucked it up behind that hedge and turned the lights off.'

Cadan squinted around him. 'We're in the middle of nowhere.'

'Which is what makes it a good place for a kidnapper to collect a ransom,' Loveday said, keeping her voice down.

'What are we supposed to do now?' She knew Cadan was frowning at her.

'Let's get a bit closer to the church.' She nodded ahead. 'It's there. We need to keep our heads down now and find a good spot. If Elise puts her car lights on again we don't want to be seen.'

They squatted down behind a bush, keeping the shadowy shape of the church in sight. If Loveday had figured this out correctly it should take Nils another half hour to reach here. It was twenty minutes later when the car's headlights appeared. Cadan grabbed her arm. 'My God, you were right, Loveday. It's him! It's Nils!'

Loveday shushed him and held her breath as the sleek wine-coloured Jaguar passed them and turned into the church car park. She was imagining how nervous Nils Olsen must now be feeling. Was his daughter here? Was she waiting somewhere nearby ready to be released as soon as he left the ransom? Could she actually be inside the church?

They heard the man get out of his car and listened to his footsteps nearing the church. Loveday crept closer until she could see him. Her heart pounded as she watched him leave a bag behind an old headstone and then go to the church door and rattle it.

'It's locked!' he yelled into the darkness. 'The church is locked! Where is Marietta? You said she'd be here. The church is locked!'

'Go back to your car, Mr Olsen,' a woman's voice cut through the night. 'Drive off and you will be told where to find your daughter.'

'No!' he roared back. 'I want Marietta brought to me right now!'

Loveday saw something move in the dark. It tore through the churchyard and grabbed the ransom.

Nils Olsen spun round. 'Marietta? Is that you?'

The shape made off across the fields with Loveday in pursuit. 'Call the police!' Loveday yelled back to Cadan. 'Call Sam!'

She could just make out the shape moving quickly ahead. It was almost at the other side of the field now. Loveday picked up her speed. She was streaking effortlessly on, blessing all those early morning jogs for her new-found stamina.

She couldn't recognize who she was chasing after but was in no doubt it was Elise. Even from this distance she could hear the woman's breathing coming in unfit gasps. She mustn't lose her! Across the field Loveday could see the woman climb a farm gate, with the bag of ransom money firmly in her grasp. She saw her pause and ducked into the hedge as the woman stared back across the dark field.

The last thing Loveday wanted was to have the woman suspect she was being followed, but Elise looked satisfied she was on her own.

Loveday hurried on, skirting the hedge until she reached the gate. There was a lane on the other side and she glimpsed Elise turning right at the end. She jogged after her, certain now that this escape route had been planned. Somewhere out here, amongst these twisting country lanes and Cornish fields, Elise had a hideaway. Is that where she was holding Marietta? Her heart leapt. Was she unwittingly leading her to Marietta?

Loveday wished now she hadn't told Cadan to wait behind at the church. She had no idea what lay ahead, or how she was going to cope with it.

CHAPTER 25

At first Loveday could see only the dark shape of buildings and thought Elise had turned off at a farmhouse but when she drew closer she realized it was a cottage. Wherever she was it felt isolated. Something rustled in the bushes ahead of her. Loveday froze, expecting Elise to pounce out at her. She held her breath, but all was still again. She tried to get her bearings. The cottage seemed to sit some way back from the lane and from what she could feel underfoot the approach to it was overgrown.

She edged along the building searching for a door and when she didn't find one decided this was an outbuilding. When she reached the corner she sensed more than saw the area opened out into a courtyard.

There was still no sign of Elise, let alone Marietta. She crept on, peering into the dark and then stopped, staring deeper into the gloom. Yes, it was definitely a flicker of light. She was so intent on the light that she didn't hear the footsteps come up behind her or sense the quick movement of the hand that had clamped over her mouth.

'Stop struggling, idiot. I'm on your side,' a voice growled in her ear. The hand was cautiously removed and Loveday spun round with a gasp. The man staring down at her was Victor Paton!

'What are you doing here?' Loveday tried to keep her voice to a low whisper.

'Same as you. I'm here for the girl.' He was pulling her back, crouching in the undergrowth at the side of the run-down building.

'I think she's holding her in a room on the other side. We have to move fast.'

Loveday swallowed. 'You think Elise is going to move the girl?'

'We both know that's not why she's here.'

'Oh, please no!' Loveday said as she realized what he meant. Elise Clark was here to kill Marietta! She prayed they weren't already too late.

'What can we do?' Her voice was an urgent hiss.

'We create a distraction – at least you do.' The moon had come out, making their surroundings more visible. Victor nodded to the end of the building. 'Can you see the paint tin amongst the rubble?'

Loveday nodded.

'Well, grab it and bash it with anything you can find. Hopefully the woman will come out to see what's going on and that's when I snatch her.' He gave her a hard stare. 'Think you can do that?'

'What if she has a gun?' Loveday asked.

'Well, let's hope she hasn't. Are we doing this or what?'

'We're doing it,' Loveday said, crawling away to retrieve the paint tin and to look for a suitably stout stick to bang on it. When she'd grabbed both things she got to her feet and stood ready, waiting for his signal to cause their diversion.

As Paton's hand came down, Loveday bashed the can as loudly as she could and kept on bashing it until the door of the cottage opened cautiously. Victor Paton had pressed himself against the wall, his body tense. As Elise emerged he caught her from behind and wrestled her to the ground, wincing as she bit his hand. 'Bitch!' he yelled as Elise Clark screamed and spat at him, fighting like a wild thing to free herself. But Paton was not letting her go.

Loveday watched as they grappled with each other. There was a branch on the ground and she saw him reach for it and bring it down on the woman's head. Elise stopped struggling after that. She was lying lifeless on the ground. Paton produced a set of handcuffs from his back pocket and snapped them on the woman's wrists, locking her hands behind her back.

Loveday's hand flew to her mouth. 'You've killed her!'

Paton laughed. 'No such luck. She's just stunned. When she comes to she'll be trying to kick the hell out of us both again.' He glanced around him. 'We need to get a move on.'

'Bastard!' Elise Clark was screaming. She spat at him, fighting like a wild thing to free herself, but there was no escaping the handcuffs.

Loveday gulped before turning and rushing into the cottage, calling Marietta's name.

'In here,' the desperate voice yelled back. 'I'm in here!'

Elise hadn't bothered locking the door to the room where she'd been holding Marietta, she'd gone to investigate the noise Loveday had been making. She'd probably thought it was enough that the girl was tied up.

Loveday rushed in and dropped to her knees beside the weeping girl. She put her arms around her. 'Hush now, Marietta. You're safe now. It's all over.'

Victor Paton appeared at the door, his hand bleeding from where Elise had bitten him. At the sight of him Marietta cowered, her eyes wide with fear.

'Don't worry,' Loveday soothed. 'He's on our side. Let's get you out of here.'

Victor Paton bent down to untie Marietta and help her to her feet. 'I know two people who will be very pleased to see you again,' he said. 'Can you walk?'

'Not very well,' Marietta said shakily. 'Can you help me?'

Loveday got to her feet and put an arm around the girl as Victor Paton supported her from the other side.

'Call the police and tell them we have Marietta,' he instructed as they made their way past the motionless shape of Elise.

'What have you done to her?' Loveday said.

'Only a tap on the head. Elise will be fine when she comes to.' Victor was leading Marietta away from the cottage. 'We'll put her in my car,' he said. 'It's over there in the trees.'

Loveday nodded. 'Let me help you,' she said, stumbling with them towards the grey Ford Astra she could now see parked in a clearing. The girl allowed them to put her into the rear of the vehicle. 'You're safe now,' Loveday soothed, hoping she sounded reassuring as she closed the car door. She slipped her mobile phone from her pocket but there was no signal. Victor Paton was starting the car. 'What are you doing?' she demanded, rushing forward to batter on the driver's half-open window. 'Marietta needs medical help. We should wait for the police.'

'I *am* the police, remember? Once a copper always a copper.' He was grinning at her. He tilted his head and called back to Marietta, 'I promised your parents I would get you safely home and I plan to do exactly that. Now let's get you away from this place.'

Loveday thought Marietta looked to be in a state of collapse, but she seemed more than willing to trust this man. She saw the girl give an exhausted nod and the word *'Yes'* trembled out. *'Please take me home.'*

Loveday watched helplessly as Victor Paton's car drove away, praying she had not just allowed Marietta to be kidnapped for a second time. She put her hands to her head. What was going on? She yanked out her phone again, shaking it, willing it to work, but there was still no reception. And there was no sign of Sam!

Maybe there had been no phone service from the church either. What if Cadan hadn't been able to contact the police? They were in the middle of nowhere. Would he think to race back to the campsite they had passed? Surely he and Nils could call for help from there?

On the ground behind her Elise was beginning to regain consciousness. She heard her moan. 'I'm sorry he knocked you out,' she said. 'But you did rather ask for it.'

'How stupid are you?' the woman yelled at her. 'You do know you've see the last of your detective pal? He'll grab the ransom and be off.'

The ransom! Loveday had forgotten about that. Victor hadn't taken the bag with him. The cash must still be here at the cottage.

She turned on Elise. 'What have you done with the Olsens' money?'

'Money?' The woman gave a sickening laugh. 'There was no money. The bag was full of paper notes. The Olsens fooled all of us!'

Loveday shone the torch on Elise's face. It was contorted with rage. She was glaring into the beam of light. 'Don't you understand? Chrissie died for nothing. I killed her and we still didn't get the cash.'

Angry tears were spilling down the woman's cheeks. 'That was to fund our new life. It was all planned. Once we got the cash we would leave Cornwall behind and move to this place I found in France.'

Loveday stared down at her. 'I don't understand. If you were planning a new life with Chrissie why did you kill her?'

The woman glared up at her, as though not understanding her stupidity. 'Because she let me down, of course. She wanted to pack it all in. She wanted to release the girl and walk away. Surely even someone as thick as you can see I couldn't let that happen.'

A splinter of ice shot through Loveday as the significance of what Elise was saying dawned on her. She swallowed back the lump in her throat. 'You never were going to release Marietta, were you?'

Elise's face twisted into a chilling smile. 'What do you think?'

Loveday couldn't bear being in this appalling woman's presence a second longer. She turned and began to move away when the rasping voice stopped her.

'I killed the Rebecca woman too,' Elise boasted. 'She thought she was too good for me. I was sick of all the airs and graces she gave herself.'

Loveday rounded on her, eyes blazing. 'You killed Rebecca? But why?'

'She rejected me. I didn't want a long, serious relationship. I had Chrissie for that. All I wanted was a fling, but I wasn't good enough for high and mighty Rebecca Monteith.'

Loveday shook her head in disbelief. 'So you killed her,' she said, her voice trembling.

'It was Victor who told me where to find her.' The sickening smile was back. 'It's amazing what you can learn from pillow talk.' She was watching Loveday for a reaction, but she'd turned her back on the woman again. It didn't stop Elise talking. She appeared to be getting some cruel pleasure from telling her story.

'Victor told me he'd been working for Rebecca,' she said. 'Something about trying to discover if Marietta was her daughter. Anyway, he'd arranged to go to her hotel room in Truro to give his report. I thought I could kill two birds with one stone, if you know what I mean. I could get rid of the woman who had rejected me and let the odious private eye get the blame. It was perfect!'

'But Victor didn't get the blame, did he,' Loveday said. 'The police believed him when he said he hadn't killed Rebecca.'

Elise gave a heavy sigh. 'Well, that's how stupid cops are,' she said.

CHAPTER 26

The Lexus screeched past Cadan and came to a halt in front of the church.

'Where is Loveday?' Sam demanded, throwing open the car door and crossing the space between them in four urgent strides. Will chased after him.

'I don't know!' Cadan's voice was full of panic. 'She tore off after Elise, at least that's who I think it was. It was difficult to tell in the dark and it all happened so fast.'

He stared at Sam with frightened eyes. 'You have to find her.'

Will raised his arms, trying to calm the situation as Nils Olsen joined them. 'Let's all chill out a bit.' He turned to Cadan. 'Tell us exactly what happened.'

Cadan pushed his hands through his hair as he paced back and forward. 'We were following Elise. It was all under control. Loveday had worked out she was meeting Nils here.'

Nils Olsen gave a hopeless shrug. 'I thought I was doing the right thing.'

'OK,' Sam said. He was struggling to stay calm. All he could think about was that Loveday was out there somewhere chasing after a woman who had already killed one, perhaps two women.

For all he knew Marietta Olsen could already be her third murder victim.

He reminded himself he was a professional and being this negative wasn't helping. He had to get back into police mode. 'Call for backup, Will. We need to comb these fields. Elise Clark and Loveday are out there somewhere and we have to find them.'

'What about Marietta?' Cadan demanded. 'She could be out there too.'

'Please find my daughter,' Nils Olsen cut in, his voice pleading.

'If she's around here we will find her.' Sam turned to his sergeant. 'You stay here with Nils and wait for backup. You know what to do.' He went to his car and found a couple of torches in the glove compartment. 'You come with me, Cadan. I want you to show me exactly where Loveday went.'

They squeezed through the gap in the hedge and emerged into a field. He handed Cadan a torch. 'Which way?'

Cadan pointed ahead. 'That way, I think.'

The beam of the torch indicated the field was larger than Sam had thought. 'I think we should go straight across,' Cadan said. 'It makes sense that Elise would have been trying to escape that way.'

Sam moved the torch around and the beam caught something white in the grass. 'What's that?' He picked up his pace until he reached the article and bent to retrieve it. 'It's Loveday's notebook.'

'D'you think she dropped it on purpose?' Cadan said.

'Maybe,' Sam said under his breath, staring into the dark. 'We need to keep going.'

They were running across the field now, their torches showing a gate on the far side.

'Look!' Cadan said. There's something there. He trained his torch on the item as Sam bent to snatch it up. 'It's Loveday's scarf,' he said. 'It's the one I gave her at Christmas.'

'So they definitely came this way,' Cadan said.

Somewhere close by they heard a car starting up. Sam put his hand on Cadan's sleeve, telling him not to move. Both men stood by the gate, straining to hear. It was definitely a car. They could hear the sound of its tyres on a hard surface. And then they saw the light. The beam from the vehicle's headlights appeared from some concealed entrance about a hundred yards to their left. Now they could see the red tail lights and knew the vehicle was being driven away from them.

A dozen possibilities about what the driver of the car was doing out at this time of night raced through Sam's head. If it was Elise they could be too late to save Loveday – or she could have been bundled up in the boot of that car.

The weight of nausea in the pit of his stomach made him want to throw up, but he had no time for that. 'Come on, Cadan,' he said as he levered himself over the fence. 'Run!'

They raced along the lane searching for the place where the car had emerged. And then they found it – a cottage set back from the lane.

Sam put a finger to his mouth, silencing Cadan, and listened. He could hear voices. His heart was racing. He indicated they should turn the torches off. They crept on silently, following the voices. At the corner of the building the area opened into a courtyard. At first the only person Sam could see was the shadowy outline of a woman on the ground. He stifled a gasp. She was manacled. It had to be Loveday.

He and Cadan began to edge forward when a voice behind them said, 'Don't move. I'm armed!'

Sam wheeled round and stared into her face in the darkness. 'Loveday? Is that you?'

'Sam!' She threw herself into his arms. 'Oh, Sam!' He smothered her in kisses, stroking her hair. 'Are you OK? She hasn't hurt you?'

'No, I'm fine. Everything's fine now you're here.'

'What about Marietta?' Cadan shouted. 'Where is she? We saw a car leave.'

'That was Victor Paton,' Loveday said. 'He's taking Marietta back to her parents.'

'She's alive? Marietta's alive?' Cadan's voice shook with emotion as his hand went out, reaching for the stone wall of the cottage to steady himself.

Loveday touched his arm. 'She's a bit shaken, and she will need some loving care, but I don't think she's been physically harmed.'

Sam was frowning. 'What do you mean, taking Marietta back to her parents? Nils is back at the church.'

'I know,' Loveday said. 'I think Victor has struck up some deal with the Olsens where he collects a reward for returning Marietta to them.'

Sam blew out his cheeks and shook his head in disbelief as he reached into his pocket for his phone.

WILL ARRIVED in Sam's Lexus with Nils Olsen in the passenger seat.

'Is Marietta here?' He sounded frantic as he rushed towards them. 'Have you found my daughter?'

Loveday reached out to him, but Sam's frown warned her to say nothing of what had happened. Victor Paton was like a loose cannon. They had no idea what he would do with the girl.

'Bear with us, Mr Olsen. We believe your daughter was here.'

'Was here!' The man's eyes were bulging from his head. 'What do you mean *was here*? Where is she? Where is Marietta?'

'Please try to stay calm, Mr Olsen.' But the man's stare went to the trussed-up shape of Elise on the ground. 'Who's that? Is she the one that took my daughter?' It was still dark, but Loveday could see the hatred in the man's eyes as he flew at her. But Will was too quick for him and wrestled him to the ground, sitting on his legs until he had calmed down. 'You must let us deal with this, sir.'

'Keep an eye on him, Loveday,' Sam ordered as he helped his sergeant bundle Elise Clark into his Lexus. Nils Olsen was struggling to his feet when his mobile phone rang. Loveday wondered why he was getting reception when she couldn't. She saw the man's face light up. 'What!' he shouted into the phone. 'Is she all right?' His hand was shaking.

'What's happened?' She stared at him.

'It's Marietta!' His shocked eyes went from her to Cadan. 'She's back!'

Cadan grabbed the phone. 'It's Cadan Tremayne. Can you repeat what you told Mr Olsen?' His face broke into a wide smile. 'Can I speak to her?' The smile continued as he listened. 'OK, but I'm coming over. Tell Marietta I'm coming!'

Sam and Will were striding back. Nils Olsen rushed towards them, grabbing their hands and shaking them vigorously. 'Marietta's back,' he kept repeating. 'She's back!'

Sam had already commandeered Olsen's phone. Loveday could hear his calm voice questioning Giselle.

'Are you and Marietta on your own there?' he asked. A pause. 'That's good. How is Marietta?' Another pause while he listened to Giselle. He nodded. 'I'm not surprised. She's been through a terrible ordeal. I want you to stay there in the hotel room, both of you. Do you understand? I'm calling for an ambulance. Marietta needs to be checked over. There will also be an officer with you shortly. Is that OK, Mrs Olsen?'

He smiled at the phone as she answered him. 'It's no problem,' he said.

Will was by his side. He was holding out his hands, waiting for an explanation of how Marietta had returned. Sam met Loveday's eyes. 'You were right. It was Victor Paton. I didn't want to question Mrs Olsen too much on the phone, but it seems she answered a knock on the door of their hotel room and Victor

Paton was standing there with Marietta. He handed her over and left.'

Will screwed up his face. 'What? Just like that?'

'Not exactly,' Sam said, levelling a look at Nils Olsen. 'What do you have to tell us, Mr Olsen?'

The man's smiling face became serious. 'Mr Paton came to see us. It was after we got the call from the kidnappers. He said he was ex Special Branch and not to trust the kidnappers. He said they would never release Marietta but he was going to get her back for us.'

'And you believed him?' Cadan was giving him an incredulous look.

Nils Olsen swallowed hard again. 'Our heads were all over the place. We didn't know what to do. Mr Paton told us we would never see our daughter again if we handed over the ransom to the kidnappers.' His bottom lip trembled. 'He said they would kill her.'

He took a sharp breath and looked around the four faces.

'Mr Paton said we had to follow their instructions except not to take the money. We'd been buying all the local newspapers in case there was any news the police were keeping from us. He helped us to cut them up and bundle them together so that they looked like a bag bank notes.'

'And he did all this out of the goodness of his heart?' Will asked.

Nils Olsen looked away. 'Not exactly. He said he would return Marietta to us, but he wanted a £100,000 reward. We already had the ransom money in the room safe, perhaps he knew that, I don't know. He said we could trust him because he wouldn't collect the reward unless he brought Marietta back.' Nils shook his head. 'So we trusted him. What choice did we have?'

'You could have called the police,' Sam cut in quickly.

Nils shook his head. 'You know we couldn't do that, not after the last time.'

They could see the lights of the police vehicles coming up the lane. Loveday wondered where they were all going to park. Elise Clark was still handcuffed and protesting in the back of Sam's car. Hissing and spitting she was transferred to a police car that was instantly dispatched to the station in Truro.

Scene of Crime officers were beginning to erect powerful spotlights.

'I need you and Cadan to go back to the station,' Sam said, turning to Loveday. 'You both have a lot of explaining to do.'

'I'll drop in at the station once I've seen Marietta,' Cadan said. 'Loveday's car's back at the church.'

Sam narrowed his eyes. 'I think we'll do it the other way round. Questions first and then you can see Marietta.' He held out a hand. 'Give me your car keys, Loveday. I'll get someone to drive it to the station for you.'

Loveday frowned at him from under her eyebrows. She didn't appreciate being told what to do, not even by Sam.

'That won't be necessary, Sam. If you can arrange a lift back to the church, I can drive Cadan and myself to Truro.'

Sam gave her an unsure look.

'Oh, for heaven's sake, Sam. We're not going to run away.' She shot Cadan a look. 'Tell him, Cadan.'

Cadan shrugged. 'I just want to see Marietta. Can we get on with this?'

CHAPTER 27

'Can you drop me off at my car in Penzance?' Cadan requested as Loveday started the Clio and they began to move away from the church. There seemed to be as much police activity here as at the cottage site across the field.

'I think Sam wanted us to go straight to the station,' she said, concentrating on the restricted vision she had of the dark road ahead.

'But Sam didn't know my car was in Penzance. It doesn't make sense to drive past it and then for me to have to come all the way back here from Truro to collect it.'

Loveday couldn't deny it made sense, but she knew as soon as Cadan was in his car he would shoot off to see Marietta. Sam had trusted her to get him to the police station for their interview.

'OK, a pact,' she said, glancing at the dashboard clock. It was almost 7.30. Promise me you will be at the station in Truro by 9 o'clock.' She could sense Cadan smiling beside her. He leaned forward and gave her a peck on the cheek. 'You're a star, Loveday. I won't let you down,' he said.

It didn't take long to reach the auction house car park in Penzance. The Clio's headlights picked out Cadan's smart sports car in the far corner. Loveday pulled alongside it and he jumped out.

'Give Marietta my love,' she called after him, grinning, as he sprinted for his car.

LOVEDAY SENSED the mood of celebration as soon as she walked into the police station. Clearly the news of Marietta's release and the capture of Elise Clark had filtered back. She was shown into one of the ground-floor interview rooms and given a cup of coffee as she waited for Sam's arrival.

She hadn't expected him to walk in for at least another hour, which would have given Cadan plenty of time to get there, but he surprised her by turning up with DC Malcolm Carter ten minutes later.

'OK, Loveday,' he said, sitting down with a sigh. 'Where is he?'

'Cadan will be here directly,' she said, giving him an innocent stare. 'I dropped him off in Penzance to collect his car. He understands the importance of this interview.' Her eyes went to the wall clock. 'He's probably trying to find a space in the car park as we speak.'

Loveday thought she detected Sam's mouth quirk. His young colleague was certainly smiling.

'But never mind Cadan. How is Marietta?' she asked.

'Amanda is with her and Giselle at the hospital. She doesn't appear to have been physically hurt, but she is traumatized. The important thing is that she's safe.'

'I'm so glad, that's just brilliant,' Loveday said, meeting Sam's eyes. 'Now what do you want to know?'

'If you could start at the beginning, please,' Sam said, checking the interview was being recorded.

Loveday described going to Penzance to meet Cadan after he'd rung her. She repeated everything she could remember about Cadan's description of how he had stood outside the door of the Olsens' hotel room and heard Giselle's conversation with the kidnapper, who they now knew was Elise Clark.

Sam frowned. 'Surely he could hear only one side of the conversation?'

'Actually no,' Loveday explained. 'According to Cadan, Giselle put the call on hands free, so Nils could hear the kidnapper's instructions.' She looked up. 'He actually recorded it on his own phone. He played it back for me. It wasn't all that clear, but you got the gist of what was being said.'

She had their full attention. Loveday leaned forward. 'Cadan persuaded me to help him, so we parked outside the Admiral Benbow, which is where Nils Olsen had been told to go. We couldn't believe our eyes when Elise Clark turned up.' She paused. 'To cut a long story short, we followed Elise to the church. We watched Nils Olsen leave the ransom behind a headstone and saw Elise spring out to snatch it and take off across the fields.'

Sam pressed his lips together. 'Go on.'

'I followed her. I tried to leave clues for which way she'd gone.' She looked at Sam. 'Did you find my scarf and the notebook?'

Sam nodded but said nothing. He didn't want to interrupt this flow.

'It wasn't easy to keep Elise in sight once I'd climbed the gate on the far side of the field. It was more intuition leading me on. Anyway, I found myself creeping around this cottage when a hand came over my mouth.' She glanced at Sam. 'I thought it was her. I was expecting to feel a blade at my neck at any moment.' Loveday touched her neck as she spoke. 'But it was him. It was Victor Paton.'

'What happened next?' Sam said quietly.

'Victor said he was there to rescue Marietta, but we had to get Elise out of the way first. We set up a distraction and when Elise appeared, Victor smashed a branch over her head and slapped a pair of handcuffs on her.

While he was doing that I ran into the cottage to search for Marietta. She was in a terrible state. She didn't know what was happening, but she recognized me and eventually calmed down.'

Loveday sucked in her bottom lip, re-living what had happened earlier. 'I managed to get her on her feet. Victor came in to help me and the three of us stumbled outside together. Elise was on the ground unconscious. Marietta still looked terrified when she saw her and cringed away. Victor said we should put Marietta in his car, which we did. I hadn't expected him to drive away leaving me with the mad woman.'

She looked up at Sam. 'That's basically what happened, and then you turned up with Cadan.'

There was a knock on the door as Loveday finished speaking and a young female officer looked in. 'Mr Tremayne is here, sir. I've put him in Interview Room Two.'

Loveday sat back, smiling. Cadan hadn't let her down after all.

LOVEDAY WAS EXHAUSTED as she drove back to Marazion that night. She could see the cottage lights were on as she turned into the drive. Her first thought was that Sam had managed to get away from the station early and had somehow got home before her, but his car wasn't there. When she left him at the police station in Truro he'd been about to interview Cadan. She parked up, deciding it must be Cassie who was in the cottage. She'd called her earlier with the news Marietta had been found safe and well. Knowing Cassie, she'd probably popped in to put a casserole in the oven for her and Sam.

But it wasn't her friend who was waiting for her when she walked into the kitchen. She stared at her uninvited guest.

'Victor Paton!'

He raised his hands in a placating gesture. 'Don't panic. I'm here to help you and your boyfriend.'

Loveday narrowed her eyes at him. 'How did you get in?'

'A window at the back. It was open.'

'No, it wasn't. We're not in the habit of leaving the cottage unsecured.'

'All right.' The placating hands came up again. 'I picked the lock.'

'You did what?'

'Don't get your knickers in a twist, sweetheart. I didn't damage it.'

Loveday glared at him. She didn't know what incensed her most, this man breaking into her and Sam's home, or him calling her sweetheart.

Out of the corner of her eye she could see the sitting room lamps had been turned on. She backed away from the man to glance into the room, half expecting to see it had been vandalized, but everything was in order and a cheery fire burned in the grate.

'I took the liberty of lighting it.' Victor grinned, following Loveday into the room. 'Hope you don't mind.'

The audacity of the man was blowing her away. She spun round, confronting him. 'You'd better start talking before I call the police.'

'No need to do that, I told you. I'm here to help.'

'Help with what?' Loveday was still glaring at him.

'Call it tying up the loose ends. I know your bloke will want to speak to me.'

'Speak to you? I expect he'll want to arrest you.'

Victor shrugged. 'Arrest me for what? I haven't committed any crime. I didn't kidnap the girl. I'm the one who rescued her…remember?'

'I think we both did that,' Loveday said.

Victor smiled. 'You played your part. You're a smart lady. I hope your boyfriend appreciates you.'

'He does,' the voice from the door said. At the sight of Sam coming into the room Loveday jumped up and ran to him.

'Mr Paton has been explaining how he hasn't done anything wrong,' she said.

Sam cocked an eyebrow at the man. 'I might dispute that.'

'It's not a crime to collect a ransom.' Victor smiled at them.

'But extortion is,' Sam said. 'You extorted £100,000 from a vulnerable couple.'

'Is that what they're saying? It's strange because the last time I saw Mrs Olsen she was more than happy to hand over the reward. I got their daughter back for them.'

Sam rolled his eyes to the ceiling. 'Why are you here, Paton?'

'I'm here to help you, Sam.' He turned to Loveday. 'I think this lovely lady was about to offer me a drink.'

Loveday shot a look to Sam and he nodded. 'Maybe we could all do with a drink. Sit down, Loveday. I'll get them.'

Victor was about to lower himself into one of the two fireside chairs when Loveday stopped him. 'Not there,' she said. 'That's Sam's chair, and the other one's mine.' She nodded to the sofa. 'You can park yourself over there.'

The man's laconic smile never left his face as sat down on the sofa.

Sam returned with three glasses of whisky on a tray.

Victor Paton sipped his drink, his face registering approval.

'Well, go on,' Sam said, settling into his chair. 'We're waiting.'

Victor took another sip of his whisky, savouring it. His slow smile went from one to the other. 'I've had my eye on the Clark woman from the beginning.'

It was on the tip of Loveday's tongue to remind him he'd slept with the woman, but she stayed silent.

'After the girl was abducted I started following her, but her life was so boring and predictable that I almost gave up. And then I saw her with the biker woman. Something was going on there and I needed to find out what that was.' He drained his glass and put it on the table next to him. 'I wasn't expecting her to be murdered. I suppose it made me lose my concentration. Elise had disappeared. She wasn't in her flat in Falmouth and she hadn't turned up for her morning job at the college or later at the pub.

I was on my way to see the Olsens to offer my services to find their daughter.'

Sam frowned. 'But you didn't know where Marietta was.'

'No, but I was sure Elise did. All I had to do was to track the woman down. I was confident she would eventually lead me to the girl.'

Loveday's attention was fixed on the man's face.

'Carry on, Paton,' Sam said.

'Like I said, I was on my way to see the Olsens when I spotted Elise in a telephone kiosk in Lemon Quay. I didn't know then, but I guess that was her contacting the Olsens.

I watched her cross the square and get into a little Mini. I was parked nearby so I followed her. At first I thought she had spotted me and was leading me on a wild goose chase, but I stuck with her and eventually ended up at this old cottage off that cross-country road to St Ives.

I didn't actually see Marietta, but I could hear her. She was yelling at Elise to release her.'

Loveday was on the edge of her seat. 'Are you telling us you found Marietta and left her there?'

She looked at Sam. He had fury written all over his face, but she knew he would say nothing. It would be important not to interrupt the man's story.

'I had to leave her there. It was the only way my plan would work.'

'But Elise might have killed her!' Loveday was trying not to yell at the man.

'It was a chance I had to take. I got back to the Olsens' hotel in double quick time.' He swallowed. 'It took a lot of persuasion to get them to trust me. They'd been told to take the £500,000 ransom to the Admiral Benbow in Penzance. I told them not to do that and helped them make up bundles of fake money using old newspapers. Then I got myself off to Penzance.'

'You were at the Admiral Benbow?' Loveday said. 'I didn't see you.'

'That's because I'm good at what I do.' He raised an eyebrow. 'I wasn't expecting you and Tremayne to turn up though. You could have sabotaged the whole thing bungling in like that.'

'We were savvy enough to follow Elise and not the money,' Loveday said.

'Yeah, I cursed you when I saw what you were doing.'

Loveday blinked. 'You couldn't have been following Elise. We would have spotted you.'

'But you didn't,' Victor said. 'When we got to the church I realized what was going to happen. Elise was planning to snatch the ransom and leg it across the fields to the cottage where she was holding Marietta. There wasn't time to think about it. I had parked back up on the road. I scampered along the lane in the dark and got into the car. I waited until I saw the lights of Nils' vehicle approaching. When he'd passed me and turned off to the church I eased the car into gear and moved silently away. I kept my headlights off until I was out of sight of the church and then made my way back to the main road and on to the cottage.'

He looked from one to the other. 'I planned to get Marietta away, but Elise had been quicker than I'd given her credit for.' He sighed. 'And then Miss Marple here turned up.'

Loveday was furious to realize she was blushing.

Victor was making moves to leave.

'You're not letting him go?' The man's arrogant smile was irritating Loveday.

Sam shrugged. 'What he did may not have been strictly ethical, but he's right. He's committed no crime.' He rounded on Victor. 'That doesn't mean you are off the hook, Paton. I'll be watching you and if you put a foot wrong I'll be down on you like a ton of bricks.'

Victor reached the door and turned, grinning at them. 'You'll have to catch me first.'

CHAPTER 28

Sam got up as the cottage door closed and went to the window to watch Victor Paton walk arrogantly away. He was smiling.

'You're up to something, Sam Kitto,' Loveday said. 'What's going on?' He came back into the room with the bottle of malt whisky. 'Well…' she said. 'Tell me.'

Sam poured a finger of whisky into each of their glasses and handed one to Loveday.

'There's no evidence Paton used force or threats, unless the Olsens tell us otherwise,' he said. 'From what I can gather, parting with £100,000 was a bargain as they saw it. They could have handed over that £500,000 ransom to Elise Clark and still not had their daughter returned to them.'

'You'll be telling me next that Victor Paton is a hero,' Loveday said.

'Hardly, but I think we all need to take a step back. Paton still has questions to answer.' He settled himself back in his chair and took a sip of the golden liquid. 'Mr Paton will find he has company when he returns to the Falmouth Detective Agency. I have two officers waiting there to invite him down to the station for a chat.'

'When did you arrange for that?' Loveday said, not able to keep the surprise from her voice.

'When I was in the kitchen fetching the whisky. I texted Will. Not that I think we can pin anything on him, but you never know.'

Loveday grinned at him and felt her tummy rumble. 'I'm suddenly starving,' she said. 'Fancy a toasted cheese sandwich?'

'Sounds great,' Sam said.

Loveday uncurled herself from the chair and headed for the kitchen, beckoning him to follow her. 'You can tell me what Cadan said while I make them.'

Sam went to the cupboard and began setting plates on a tray. 'Without going into any detail, he said more or less the same as you, tinged with more than a touch of euphoria of course.'

Loveday swung round, smiling. 'He really is delighted that Marietta is safe. I've never seen him getting so intense about anyone. I think our Cadan is in love.' She paused, cheese knife in hand. 'With someone other than himself, I mean.'

When their sandwiches were ready they took them through to the sitting room, together with the mugs of hot chocolate Sam had made.

'When will you interview Elise?' she asked.

'First thing in the morning. She isn't going anywhere. I wanted to leave her to cool off before the formal interview.'

'Will I have to give evidence in court?' Loveday asked.

Sam wiped the toast crumbs from his mouth before answering. 'That depends on whether Elise pleads guilty or not.'

Loveday had put her mobile phone on the little table and they both looked up as it pinged. She picked it up. 'It's a reminder I put in the diary.' She smiled. 'Merrick and Connie are back from their honeymoon tomorrow.'

LOVEDAY HAD GONE into the office early. She'd spent most of the week mopping up loose ends to make sure the magazine was ready for the publishers.

'Congratulations, Loveday, it's a great edition,' Keri said, looking over her shoulder as she scanned the pages on the computer screen. 'Merrick will be delighted.'

Loveday nodded. 'I think he will. It's been a great team effort.' Despite two murders, a kidnapping and all the other distractions she'd had to deal with over recent days they had produced another good edition of *Cornish Folk*.

She wondered about emailing the pages to him and decided against it. He and Connie would still be bathed in rosy glow memories of their honeymoon. They wouldn't appreciate being brought back to earth with a bump…not yet.

Her eyes went to the clock. It was almost noon. The happy couple would be home by now.

Keri was also checking the time. 'Would you mind if I take an early lunch? Ben sold two paintings yesterday and he's treating me.'

'Of course not, Keri.' Loveday beamed across the desk at her. 'You go. That's great news. Give Ben a hug from me.'

'That will really make his day.' Keri laughed, giving Loveday a backward wave as she left the office.

It was another twenty minutes before her phone buzzed an alert that a text had arrived. It was from Merrick.

'We're back! Molly has made a huge buffet lunch. Care to join us?'
She texted back:
'Welcome home! Lunch sounds lovely. Can't wait to see you two again.' She added two red hearts and immediately deleted them. Merrick would think she'd gone soppy. She'd been half wondering if she might get a call from Sam inviting her for a lunchtime drink, but none had arrived. He was probably still busy with Elise Clark's interview.

A wave of excitement tingled through her as she approached

Morvah. It felt good being back at the Tremayne home. Cadan's green sports car was parked at the side of the house and she drew alongside it. She hoped he hadn't already burdened Merrick and Connie with details of the murders and Marietta's kidnapping.

Molly's wide grin was welcoming as she answered the door and shepherded Loveday into the vast drawing room. Merrick came striding to meet her, arms outstretched.

'Well,' Loveday said, her gaze travelling to an attractively tanned Connie. 'No need to ask how you two are. Welcome home.' She went to hug Connie. She hadn't at first noticed Marietta sitting shyly between a happy looking Cadan and Edward Tremayne She rushed forward to hug her too. 'Marietta!' Her eyes travelled over the girl, searching for any sign of injuries. There was none as far as she could see. 'It's wonderful to see you again.'

She wasn't aware of the confused look that passed between Merrick and Connie.

Behind her the door opened and to Loveday's surprise, Sam came striding into the room. Merrick went to greet him. 'Glad you could make it, Sam,' he said, putting a hand on his shoulder. Sam smiled across to Connie. Loveday saw his eyebrow go up as he spotted Marietta. She reached for his hand and pulled him down onto the sofa beside her, smiling across the room to Merrick and Connie. 'So are you going to tell us about the fabulous time you've both clearly had?'

'All in good time,' Merrick said. 'We gather quite a lot has been happening here in our absence.'

Loveday suppressed a frown. She hadn't wanted to spoil her friends' homecoming with such shocking revelations of what had been happening in their absence. She was annoyed with Cadan for burdening them with such grim news when they had only just set foot back in Morvah again. She could tell by Sam's expression that he wasn't any more impressed than she was.

Merrick had got to his feet. 'Connie and I go on holiday for a few days and all this happens while we're away.' He held open his arms.

Loveday was trying not to sigh. She'd wanted the couple's happy glow to last a bit longer.

'I'm so sorry, Merrick. Cadan shouldn't have told you like this.'

'I agree,' Merrick said. 'He should have phoned us, but then maybe he thought he would have been pinching our limelight.'

Loveday slid Sam a bewildered look. She wasn't sure what Merrick was talking about, but she sensed she should say no more until this had been made clear.

Cadan had reached for Marietta's hand. They were gazing into each other's eyes as though they shared a special secret.

And then it dawned on her. 'You're engaged!' she cried.

Marietta held out her hand and the diamond on her finger glinted.

Loveday reached forward to hug the girl again. 'I've no idea how you managed to do all this so quickly, Cadan, but congratulations. I'm so happy for you.'

Molly had reappeared with a tray of glasses. Merrick retrieved a champagne bottle from the ice bucket he had secreted on a table in the corner.

'Fetch a glass for yourself too, Molly. I want everyone to toast the happy couple.'

Molly looked unsure, but Edward nodded. 'Yes, please join us, Molly,' he said.

Merrick filled the glasses and handed them round. 'To Cadan and Marietta,' he said, raising his glass.

'To Merrick and Connie,' Cadan said. 'May you have a long and happy life together, just as Marietta and I plan to do.' Everyone smiled and echoed the sentiments.

'Well,' Merrick said, settling himself down beside his new wife. 'Have we missed anything else while we've been away?'

Loveday and Sam exchanged a look.

Marietta leaned forward and kissed Cadan gently on the mouth. 'Nothing that can't wait,' she murmured.

Dear reader,

If you enjoyed the book you could make this author very happy by spending a few minutes to leave an honest review on the site where you bought it.

Thank you.

ALSO BY RENA GEORGE

THE LOVEDAY MYSTERIES

A Cornish Revenge

A Cornish Kidnapping

A Cornish Vengeance

A Cornish Obsession

A Cornish Malice

A Cornish Betrayal

A Cornish Deception

A Cornish Ransom

THE MELLIN COVE TRILOGY

Danger at Mellin Cove

Mistress of Mellin Cove

Secrets of Mellin Cove

- also –

Highland Heart

Inherit the Dream

Fire in the Blood

Where Moonbeams Dance

A Moment Like This

Printed in Great Britain
by Amazon